The Things We Do for Love

FIVE STAR

Other Five Star Titles by Glenda Sanders:

Home Again

The Things We Do for Love

GLENDA SANDERS

Five Star
Unity, Maine

All the characters in this book are fictitious. Any resemblance to actual persons, living or dead, is purely coincidental.

Five Star Romance Series.
Published in 2001 in conjunction with Glenda Sanders.

The text of this edition is unabridged.

Set in 11 pt. Plantin by Minnie B. Raven.

Printed in the United States on permanent paper.

Library of Congress Cataloging-in-Publication Data

Sanders, Glenda, 1948–
The things we do for love / Glenda Sanders.
p. cm.
ISBN 0-7862-3130-0 (hc : alk. paper)
1. Unemployed — Fiction. 2. Florida — Fiction.
3. Large type books. I. Title.
PS3561.A33 T48 2001
813′.54—dc21 00-066347

The Things We Do for Love

Chapter One

"Won't be able to make it? *He won't be able to make it?* Gretchen, the show is tomorrow. How can he possibly back out on such short notice?"

"I know this imposes a hardship on you, but our agency will do everything we can to provide another model." Gretchen Hobart's voice was cool in contrast to the note of hysteria that tinged Shelby Thurston's. But then, Gretchen was not the one with her head on a chopping block.

"You don't have anyone suitable available," Shelby said, trying not to be intimidated by the older woman's poise and confidence. "I looked through your books, remember? There were only three possible candidates, and two of them were already booked. You promised me Rafe Owens, and Rafe Owens agreed to come. Our costumer fitted the costume to him. He can't back out at this late date."

Gretchen's indulgent chuckle grated on Shelby's nerves, and she spoke as to a child. "I admit that Rafe's decision might be a little unprofessional."

Shelby sniffed indignantly. "A *little* unprofessional?"

"You must be realistic, Shelby. He was offered a featured role in *Miami Vice.* Was he supposed to give that up for a trade show?"

"He could have flown down after the show."

"It was today or no go," Gretchen said. "I'm terribly sorry, Shelby, but that's the way things happen in this business. If you'd like to come over and go through our book again . . ."

"No, thank you, Gretchen," Shelby said icily, hoping the chill in her voice would at least frost the seams of Gretchen's steel armor. Silently she vowed never, ever to do business with Gretchen's agency again. Provided, of course, that she remained in a position to do business with *any*body's agency after tomorrow, which she probably wouldn't if she didn't find a man—and the right sort of man—between now and eight o'clock tomorrow morning.

After pouring herself a fresh cup of coffee, she settled back into the worn, comfortable chair behind her desk, flipped open her spiral organizer and began calling other talent agencies to see if any of the models she'd picked out from their photo files were suddenly, miraculously free for the weekend. Two hours later, dejected, she sighed wearily and switched on her answering machine. It was past two o'clock and she hadn't even had lunch. Maybe a change of scenery and a little nourishment would provide a divine revelation about where to find the man she needed.

She was too preoccupied to notice what she was piling onto her plate at the salad bar, too worried to appreciate the freshness of the crisp vegetables or taste the delicate blend of seasonings in the salads she'd selected.

Finding men had never been a major concern for Shelby. Men always seemed to find her—enough men, at any rate, to keep her social life on an even keel. The fact that she was a Thurston—one of *the* Thurstons—seemed to fascinate a lot of men, too, but she judiciously tried to avoid the ones she perceived to be more interested in her pedigree than her personality.

Shelby never understood why people were so interested in her background. The Thurstons were an important family in Orlando, but it wasn't as though they'd come over on the *Mayflower*. They were Florida landed gentry, their fortune accumulated through the land, thanks to the presence of mind of Great-great-granddaddy Thurston, who had diversified his holdings among orchards, beef cattle and horse breeding, and her grandfather, who had discovered a new kind of land revenue during the post-Disney World boom.

As Shelby left the restaurant and got into her car, she thought of the men she knew, men who might be willing to do her a favor to save the public relations firm she'd begun on her own and that had become her badge of independence. Palmer would be perfect, but Palmer had run off to Alaska to sow his wild oats. Everyone else she could think of either wouldn't qualify or wouldn't cooperate. It was no simple favor she would be asking, after all. Visions of cruising singles' bars in search of a willing candidate filled her head.

Her balled fist struck the steering wheel of her sports car while she waited for a traffic light to change. Damn! Somewhere there had to be a man with the right qualifications, a man who wouldn't have to be at work on Friday and who would be eager to earn a few bucks.

Good grief! Why hadn't she thought of it before? It was worth a try. After pulling into the next filling station with a pay phone, Shelby dialed her best friend's office number. "Lacey, last year, when you were collecting unemployment, where did you go?"

"Shelby? Is that you?"

"This is important, Lacey. Where did you go?"

"To an office in Winter Park," Lacey said, and gave directions.

Austin Hastings shifted restlessly in the line that seemed never to move. His discomfort was due to more than the stuffiness of the room and his natural impatience. He did not want to be here; he still half expected to wake up and discover that the confrontation with Bruce Mason Junior had not resulted in this illogical, unjust situation. But he knew he was not asleep and that this nightmare was no dream. The knowledge he had acquired, that in business blood runs thicker than logic, still grated on raw nerve endings.

Several minutes ticked by. Austin was tempted to leave. He had a month's severance pay and a moderate savings account to live on until he found another job, which shouldn't take long. Stubbornly, though, he stuck with the line. Job hunting was a precarious process, and he was taking nothing for granted in the wake of his recent experience, not the professional associates he'd contacted from coast to coast who were supposed to be keeping an eye out for suitable openings, not even the fact that he was a good engineer with solid experience and a strong résumé. His experience with the Masons, junior and senior, had temporarily undermined his usually unshakable confidence. He *should* find a job before his reserves ran out, but in a world where a man could lose his job for insisting on excellence and opposing incompetence, anything could happen.

He was abysmally bored—until the dark-haired woman walked in. She was a looker, this one, with shoulder-length black hair, flawless skin and brown eyes filled with life. There was a haughty tilt to her chin, and her full lips seemed poised to smile at any second.

Or be kissed, he thought, and smiled at the prospect.

Slightly taller than average, she had long, shapely legs, a slender waist and full breasts shown to advantage by the low-cut blouse she was wearing with a suit that was tailored but slightly frivolous. She seemed to exude energy, an obvious enthusiasm for life. She was, at once, provocative, feminine and crisply professional, and she wore her outfit with an aplomb that announced that her only concern in fashion was finding what suited her.

She was, Austin concluded, a study of contrasts. There was a confidence in her stride, a sureness in her step that belied the anxious, almost timid, expression in her eyes as she looked around the room.

He wondered if she, too, was in shock, one of the walking wounded, unemployed through no fault of her own, a victim, perhaps, of jealousy in the workplace as he was. Her beauty could certainly inspire jealousy, and if she was intelligent, too . . .

Her eyes met his as she surveyed the room. She had caught him staring at her but refused to shy away.

For several seconds their attention remained fixed on each other. Austin was a little nonplussed by her frank perusal. It was not an overt come-hither look she was directing at him, but one of unapologetic curiosity and interest. Self-consciously he nodded in greeting, then felt a weird sensation in the pit of his stomach as she took the first step toward him. Men just didn't get so lucky.

Shelby couldn't believe her eyes. He was exactly the man she needed: tall and sturdy with a majestic bearing, olive skin that had been caressed by the sun, thick brown hair with sun-bleached highlights, large eyes under thick brows, a square face with a strong jaw and good cheekbones. She knew instinctively that his voice would be deep and imposing.

He had been watching her—appraising her was more accurate—when she first caught sight of him, and his nod gave her the courage to approach him. It was an unorthodox way to do business, but she was in a desperate situation. She'd be perfectly frank and offer him the job. It worked for producers in Hollywood drugstores; it should suffice for a desperate public relations specialist in central Florida.

He continued watching her as she walked toward him. She smiled. Mr. Perfection smiled back, and Shelby was reassured. "Excuse me," she said upon reaching him. "I'm Shelby Thurston. Here, I'll get you one of my business cards."

Why hadn't she thought to have one ready? At least they were in an easily accessible zipper pocket in her purse. She gave him a few seconds to read the card.

The Shelby Agency, he read. Projecting the best image for your business. It was certainly a new approach.

"If you're free tomorrow and through the weekend, Mr. . . ."

"Hastings. Austin Hastings," he answered, thinking she was even prettier up close. "Call me Austin."

Her lips, full and glossy, titillated his imagination as she spoke. "Great, Austin. I like working on a first-name basis. Call me Shelby."

I'd call you grandma if that's the way you wanted to play the game, he thought.

"As I was saying, Austin, if you're free tomorrow and this weekend, I have a job you'd be perfect for. It's only temporary, but the *per diem* pay is reasonable and lunches are included."

From his height advantage, the expanse of cleavage teasingly revealed by her blouse was almost unbearably provocative. "Okay," he said. He didn't give a damn about the job; he didn't even think to ask exactly how much he'd be paid; the fringe benefits were all he was concerned with.

His ready acquiescence stunned Shelby. Didn't he even want to know what the job was, what would be expected of him? Her sense of fair play told her to elaborate a little about what he would be doing, but she wasn't stupid. He was the solution to a monumental problem, and she wasn't about to run him off. “Good,” she said and smiled. “I hope you’re free the rest of the afternoon. There’s some preparation—”

“I’m all yours,” he said, and suddenly the suggestion in his voice and the way he was looking at her made her question the wisdom of involving herself with a total stranger.

Shelby’s looks often stirred men sexually; she accepted it as a fact of life. Men frequently looked at her the way Austin was looking at her now. What gave Shelby pause about Austin Hastings was the way she felt when she looked back at him. He was a disturbingly potent package of masculinity.

“I’ll, uh, wait for you near the door,” she said feeling strangely tongue-tied.

“That won’t be necessary,” he said, cupping her elbow in his hand.

“B-but . . .” she protested, even as she fell into step beside him. “What about your unemployment benefits? Don’t you want to fin—”

“I was tired of standing in that line anyway.” The papers in his hand crackled as he compressed them into a ball. He dropped them into a large trash can just outside the door of the building and turned his attention to Shelby as they reached the edge of the parking lot.

“Where to?” he asked.

“My office,” she said, not mentioning that she operated her business out of the family room of her duplex. “You can follow me.”

His smile was disarming. “To the ends of the earth, if you want.”

Shelby was surprised to find that her hands were trembling as she started her car. She had gone in search of an extraordinary man, and she had certainly found one! Now she had the uneasy feeling that she was riding a tiger she dared not dismount.

Austin's cream-and-tan Buick kept up with her easily, remaining in her rearview mirror throughout the short drive. More than once, Shelby wondered what she'd done, what insanity had prevailed upon her to put herself in the position of bringing a total stranger into her home. Imaginary headlines flashed in her mind: Local Woman Found Murdered. The accompanying story would mention that there were no signs of forced entry, leading detectives to believe that the victim knew her assailant. Her family pedigree would be mentioned along with the fact she had recently founded a public relations agency. Lacey would tell the police about her strange phone call. Perhaps witnesses would recall having seen her at the unemployment office, maybe someone would even describe the man she left with. Maybe he wouldn't get off scott free. Maybe . . .

Good grief, Shelby, can the imagination! she chided herself. He probably wouldn't present any problems a well-placed, solid kick wouldn't solve. Not that Shelby had ever had to resort to well-placed, solid kicks. She had a way of telling a man no, politely but effectively. A woman with her natural assets learned to deal with unwanted advances early on. Shelby's chest had begun developing at age eleven, and she had been perfecting her no-nonsense "no" ever since.

They entered through the side door, which led directly into her office. Shelby had decided a frankly businesslike approach would be best, and she invited him to sit down, nodding toward an armchair in front of her desk. She settled into the chair behind the desk and slid a notepad toward Austin. "Why don't you write down your name, address, phone and social security numbers and a brief employment history while I see if there are any messages on my recorder."

He picked up the pad and, disregarding the ten-for-a-dollar disposable ballpoint she'd placed on top of it, reached into his pocket and withdrew a gold-plated Cross pen and began to write.

Shelby rewound the tape on her machine and pressed playback. Lacey's voice was the first to follow a beep. "I've got to know what that cryptic phone call was all about. What kind of mischief are you up to this time, Shelby? Call me when you get a chance."

Shelby shifted in her seat as she waited for the next beep, hoping the message would be business rather than personal. It was. "Shelby, this is Caroline, from Mr. Caesar's office. He wanted to talk to you about tomorrow and make sure everything is going along okay, but he said if you weren't in, he'd just see you at the show. He's leaving early today, and it's almost four o'clock, so you don't have to return the call."

Austin had finished with the pad and placed it on her desk within reach. Shelby scanned it, noting that the address was complete, including zip code. She smiled. "What did you do at Mason Engineering?"

"I'm an engineer."

Shelby wondered if she imagined the hint of bitterness tinging his words. "I see," she said for want of a better reply. "Well, what I'm offering isn't exactly an engineering job. Have you ever, by any chance, modeled or acted?" She tried not to panic at the scowl forming on his face. "It wouldn't have to be professionally. High school or college plays, anything."

He shrugged. "Sorry."

"It doesn't matter," she said quickly. "This isn't a particularly demanding role. It just requires a nice smile and a little charm. We both know you're a charming fellow." She had tried to sound light, but her last remark seemed silly, even to Shelby. It was as if she were trying to flirt with him and had no finesse.

To cover the awkwardness she was feeling, she said quickly, "Perhaps you've heard of my client, Caesar's Office World?"

"There's one on I-4, isn't there?"

She nodded. "Their main store. There are several others. Caesar's is growing, expanding. They have three offices in Orlando, two in Tampa, one each in St. Pete and Tallahassee, and they're hoping to move into Miami next year. Mr. Caesar thought—and rightly so—that it was time Caesar did some promotion to establish its name in the marketplace, so he hired The Shelby Agency to help promote it. I did some informal market research into who usually buys office supplies and advised Mr. Caesar to zero in on those people through trade shows and exhibit booths. He agreed."

She took a deep breath before continuing, and stared Austin straight in the eye. She was sure from the look she found there that his mind was not wholly on Caesar's Office World. At the moment she didn't care why he was there, only that he was.

"Caesar's needed a gimmick," she continued, "something to distinguish it from its competitors and establish it in the minds of potential customers. That's where you come in, Austin."

Austin shifted uncomfortably in the chair. He didn't like the note of wariness that had crept into her voice. It sounded too much like she was about to deliver bad news. He had the distinct impression he was being manipulated, led into something gently. "A gimmick, you say?"

Shelby sucked in a deep breath and tried not to wince as she asked, "Have you ever had any fantasies about being Julius Caesar?"

Chapter Two

Shelby held her breath as she watched realization register on Austin's face. He might just get up and walk out, and then where would she be?

"Julius Caesar?"

Shelby grinned sheepishly. "You've got it."

It was still registering with Austin. "The Caesar who wore togas and sandals."

"Not sandals, exactly. They're called *calcei*."

"No way!"

Time for desperate measures, Shelby thought. *Begging, pleading, feminine wiles.* If he left, she was stuck. "Please do it, Austin," she said, then paused for effect before continuing. "The truth is this account is extremely important to me, and I could lose it if I don't show up with Julius Caesar tomorrow morning. I booked an actor through a legitimate agency, but he ran off to do a *Miami Vice* episode and I'm really stuck if you back out."

Austin looked into her dark, lustrous eyes, then his gaze roamed to her lovely neck and fetching cleavage. "Where is this show, and who's going to be there?"

"It's a regional meeting of the Florida Clerical Workers Association. Six hundred secretaries, clerks and bookkeepers. It opens tomorrow and runs through Saturday at the Airport Convention Center."

"All female?" he asked dubiously.

"Mostly. They're the ones who buy office supplies."

The lines in Austin's forehead deepened as he considered this information. "If I didn't think I'd run into anyone I know . . ."

"Have you left a string of broken-hearted secretaries between here and Pensacola?" Shelby asked.

Shaking his head, he chuckled self-deprecatingly. "Hardly. It's just . . ."

"You'll do it?" Shelby said, pressing her advantage.

Austin was drawn to her eyes again. They were expectant now, filled with hope. He sighed. Lord, but he was a sucker for a sad story and a pretty face. Frowning at his own vulnerability, he said, "I'll do it."

Her smile of gratitude dispelled his ambivalence. He didn't mind having a beautiful woman indebted to him. Sooner or later she might feel compelled to express her gratitude.

It was a most cheering prospect.

Trying not to show how relieved she was, Shelby stood up and walked around the desk. "Let's see if the costume fits. I think you're about the same size as the actor, so it shouldn't be a problem." Austin followed her to an antique wardrobe chest that had been converted into office storage by installing adjustable shelves. The costume was hanging on a hook on the inside of the door. Shelby unzipped the plastic bag and took out a hanger. "Here's your tunic. You can change in the bathroom."

"It's a dress," Austin said, staring at the garment disdainfully.

"It's a tunic," she corrected. "It goes under the toga to ensure . . . in case the toga slips."

Austin exhaled wearily. "I don't know about this, Shelby. I'd like to help you out, but . . ."

"No one will see you without the toga. They'll just see

your purple stripes." She stroked the elegant braid edging the neck of the tunic. "They're called *clavi,* and they're the symbol of rank and authority. Caesar was one of the greatest warriors and statesmen of all time, and *he* wore a tunic under his toga."

"Two thousand years ago," Austin replied dryly. "Shelby, *everybody* wore togas two thousand years ago."

"A man like you doesn't have to worry about what he wears," Shelby said. "Joe Namath made a panty hose commercial and that baseball player—what's his name?—made billboards in his underwear and Shakespearean actors . . ."

"So I'm supposed to be secure enough in my manhood to wear a dress in front of six-hundred women and not worry about what anyone thinks?" he asked, with an endearing grin.

Embarrassed to be caught at the manipulative game she was playing, Shelby nodded sheepishly. Touched by the blush he knew she hoped he wouldn't notice, Austin smiled. "With my manhood at stake, I think I'd better get into my tunic."

Shelby swallowed to moisten her suddenly dry throat. "Go right down that hall. The bathroom's the first door on the left." She watched him walk away carrying the tunic on the hanger: broad shoulders, trim waist, long legs, thick hair a woman could run her hands through.

She wasn't fool enough to question Austin Hasting's manhood.

Shelby's bathroom was a shrine of femininity with a fluffy bath rug, mirror-bottomed makeup trays with gold filigree sides, fancy powder shakers, and an enormous fern suspended in a basket beneath a small skylight. A hint of perfume floated in the air.

Austin felt out of place, like a hired gardener at a garden

club breakfast, and he moved gingerly, fearful of knocking something over as he undressed. After draping his shirt and pants over the antique brass-and-porcelain hook on the back of the door, he pulled the tunic over his head and adjusted it over his body. Catching sight of himself in the mirror, he cringed. Though he could see himself only from the waist up in the mirror at the vanity, his worst fears were confirmed. Tunic was just a fancy name for a dress. It capped loosely over his shoulders to form short sleeves, and hung limply just above his knees.

Above his head, the air conditioner sprang into service with a sudden whooshing sound, and an unexpected draft of air swirled around his legs, surprising him, leaving him feeling peculiarly exposed. No wonder women wore slips and panty hose and such.

He looked in the mirror at the boat neck of the tunic edged in braid. *Cutie pie,* he told the reflection derisively, and thought, *Lord, what has my penchant for a pretty face gotten me into?*

Finally, he took a deep breath and delivered himself to his persecutor. "What now?" he asked.

Shelby looked up from the papers she was reading and, catching sight of Austin, was on the verge of a giggle when he said, "Don't you dare laugh, lady."

She swallowed to maintain her composure and said, "It's not the tunic, Austin. Really it's not. It's those socks and deck shoes."

Austin looked at his feet; then at Shelby, and grinned. "I should have worn purple pumps?"

Their combined laughter was cathartic. Shelby got up and took a box from the wardrobe. "I think it's time to try these on for size."

"I wear a ten and a half," Austin said.

"Good. These are elevens. They didn't come in half sizes. Kick off your shoes and sit down. I'll lace them for you."

Austin approached the chair and began lowering himself into the seat. Abruptly he straightened again, tugging at the hem of the tunic.

"Problems?" Shelby asked, fighting back laughter.

"It rides up," Austin growled.

Shelby chuckled at his dilemma. "Just be careful to keep your knees together." She knelt next to the chair and guided his foot onto the flat sole of the boot. Lifting the long leather thong in the air and studying a printed sheet she'd taken from the plastic wrapper encasing the strings, she said, "Looks like these lace and cross routinely and tie at the top. Tell me if I pull them too tight."

Nose to shin with him, she couldn't help noticing what nice calves he had. Slim but muscular, they tapered aristocratically to his slender ankles. "We'll have to go without the socks tomorrow," she said. "You might want to make sure your nails are clipped and filed straight across."

"Yes, Mom!" he said wryly. Then he yelped, "Ouch!"

She looked at him quizzically. "Too tight?"

"No. You caught a hair."

"Sorry!" she said, loosening the thong, massaging the patch of skin under the last eyelet she'd threaded. "I'll be more care—"

Something passed between them as she looked up and their eyes met, an intangible but undeniable force, a silent but powerful jolt of sexual awareness. It reduced their existence and their relationship to each other to the most elemental of terms: he was a man, she was a woman. For an instant nothing else was relevant.

Shocked by the power of the attraction between them, they stared at each other for several seconds, speechless, unmoving, heedless of time or their surroundings.

Slowly, the realization of where they were and what they were—and were not—to each other dawned. Shelby was overcome by a feeling of lethargy as she forced her attention back to the boots. It seemed to her that her fingers were moving in slow motion as she finished lacing the first *calcei* and began the other. Even her tongue was uncooperative as she spoke. "I, uh, this shouldn't take long."

Austin's nod of acknowledgment only intensified the awkward silence, as Shelby worked on threading the thong through the eyelets. When at last she had finished, she patted the leather side of the tall, open-toed boot and said, "Why don't you walk around a bit and see how these feel."

They stood up in unison, Austin reaching down to cup his hand under her elbow to assist her. Their eyes locked as the same awareness sparked between them at the physical contact. They asked a silent question: *How are we going to handle this?*

Austin smiled, shattering the charged atmosphere, defusing the tension. Shelby returned the gesture gratefully. *They were going to play it cool.*

After circling the room a couple of times, Austin decided the fit of the boots was bearable. Shelby had taken out the toga and was studying the instructions for draping it. " 'Position gathered shoulder on left shoulder, adjusting shoulder stay comfortably and suspend End A in front from shoulder to above left foot,' " she read aloud. "Here's the shoulder. Slip your arm through here and hold this in place, and I'll tighten the strap."

When she conceived the idea of a real Caesar, sold the concept to Mr. Caesar, and ordered the custom-made costume, Shelby had not foreseen the problem of being attracted to the man she would be dressing. True, she had searched exhaustively for the right model and had appreciated the physical perfection of the one she had hired. But it had been an aesthetic appreciation, like admiring Michelangelo's *David.* With Austin, the admiration was accompanied by a rare excitement that left her slightly off kilter.

The effect Austin Hastings was having on her was unsettling. Fingers that could fly efficiently over a computer keyboard and nimbly execute intricate needlepoint designs were suddenly fumbling with a simple slide on a flat band of cotton. She decided that the clumsiness extended all the way to her brain when, after adjusting the strap to what looked like a reasonable fit, she ran her finger up and down between the strap and Austin's shoulder to test the tightness and asked guilelessly, "How does this feel?"

Austin sighed and undulated his shoulders. "Terrific. Don't stop."

"I was referring to the strap," Shelby said.

"Oh. The strap," he repeated, feigning surprise. "It's okay."

Vowing not to feed him any more ridiculous straight lines, Shelby stepped in front of Austin to check the fall of the fabric that was draped from his shoulder to his foot. Holding the undraped end of the toga in her left hand, she smoothed the folds of the material.

Austin put his hand over hers, trapping it against his chest. "That feels pretty good, too."

Too good, thought Shelby. Very gently she slid her hand from under his and reached for the instruction sheet again. Attached to the cloth she held, Austin was forced to follow closely behind her. She could feel his breath on her neck as she tried to decipher the written text and line drawings.

"Across the back now," she said, plunging her hand, with the cloth, back under his left arm and reaching around him with her right arm to pass the fabric from one hand to the other.

Bad move, she thought disgustedly as she found herself, in effect, hugging him, her chin nearly pressing against his breastbone. Why hadn't she simply walked around him? As his hands came to rest on her waist and pulled her closer to him, she became disturbingly aware that he was as physically affected by their closeness as she was.

She was embarrassed. And fascinated. Slowly she tilted her head up to look at his face, sensing that he already was looking at her. She watched, mesmerized, as he lowered his face to hers, frozen by the anticipation of his kiss. Almost too late she realized what was happening and twisted away from him. The undraped tail of the toga fell to the floor as she let go of it.

"Oh, damn!" she said. Austin put his hands on her upper arms and looked at her questioningly. She sighed, closing her eyes. Her shoulders drooped wearily. Austin lifted his right hand and touched her cheek. Shelby opened her eyes.

"Are you involved with someone?"

"No. It's . . ." *Careful,* she cautioned herself, *you need this man.* She sighed softly. "You're an attractive man, Austin, but we're going to be working together, and it could get awkward if we . . ." The sentence, left dangling, did not require completion.

Austin studied her face a moment. "Whatever you say." As frustrating as the delay might be, Austin was sure Shelby Thurston was worth a few days' wait.

She walked behind him, picked up the bottom of the toga and began draping again, pulling, pushing, patting and smoothing the cloth with her right hand as she held the instructions in her left. "I can't believe it!" she said after a long silence. "There's a patch of Velcro on your shoulder, and here's the matching patch right here. We got it right."

Turning his head in her direction, Austin caught a whiff of her perfume as she pressed the two Velcro patches together triumphantly. Several layers of toga separated them, but he still was aware of her breasts near his chest. He wanted, very badly, to wrap his arms around her again and steal the kiss she'd forestalled earlier. But he didn't want to alienate her, so he said lightly, "I don't think the Romans worried about matching up Velcro patches."

Stepping back to appraise her handiwork, Shelby answered, "The Romans had special slaves whose only duty was to drape their togas. You're stuck with me and Velcro."

No complaints, Austin thought. He said, "Does this mean if the Velcro patches don't match I can throw you to the lions?"

"If the Velcro patches don't match we start over and try again until they do match, or *Mr. Caesar* throws me to the lions," Shelby answered. "Is it comfortable? Are you going to be able to wear it all day?"

Austin shrugged. "No problem, except that I feel like a fool."

Shelby appraised him from head to toe, taking in his muscular arms tanned the color of honey, his hard calves above his tall boots, the contrast between the flowing lines of his garment and the uncompromising solidity of the man wearing it. She unconsciously took a deep breath, trying to maintain professional detachment. "You don't look like a fool," she told him flatly, and without hesitation, asked, "Are you going to be able to sit down in this getup, or will we have to wait until we're at the hall to dress you?"

Austin sat down tentatively in the leather chair. "It feels okay, but it might wrinkle."

Shelby shook her head. "This fabric is a synthetic blend. The wrinkles are supposed to shake out."

"The real Romans never had it so good."

"I think they wore wool," she said. "Can you imagine wearing wool in Italy in the summertime?"

"A sticky proposition."

"At best," Shelby agreed. She smoothed the cloth near Austin's shoulder. "I think we can get this back on you without too much trouble in the morning, don't you?"

A grin spread over Austin's face, and his eyes twinkled devilishly. "If we don't, I'll just feed you to the lions."

"I'll lie awake all night quaking in fear."

"A bit cheeky for a slave, aren't you?"

She raised her eyebrows and answered haughtily, "*I* know where the Velcro patches are."

"So when do you get me *out* of this thing?"

Shelby laughed. "Right now if you're ready. There's no need to keep it on now that we know it fits."

"Are you always so cooperative about helping men undress, or do you have a thing about togas?"

She pummeled his shoulder playfully with her fist. "Watch thy tongue, Caesar, lest it get naughty." She unwound the toga, folding it carefully as she drew it away from his body.

"Can I go get into my own clothes now?" Austin asked impatiently as she straightened the folded fabric over the hanger.

"Sure," she said. "Oh, and Austin," she called to his retreating back. He stopped, turned, arched his eyebrows expectantly. A mischievous smile spread over her face. "You might want to wear white underwear tomorrow in case you somehow get unwound."

Shelby found his blush irresistible.

Chapter Three

"You didn't say anything about a laurel wreath yesterday."

Shelby dismissed Austin's early-morning petulance with a wave of her hand. "It's no big deal. You won't even know it's there."

Dropping into a chair next to the kitchen table where Shelby waited with a comb, brush and hairpins, he grumbled, "Don't blame me if I get a Socrates complex and start spouting philosophy."

Shelby picked up the brush and pulled it through his hair. It was thick and coarse, a man's hair, she thought, enjoying the feel of it. "Is your hair curlier when it's wet?" she asked.

"Yes. I have to blow dry it to straighten it out."

"I'll be right back," she said, and dashed off, only to return a moment later with a spray bottle and an aerosol can. "I'm going to dampen your hair so it will swirl around the laurel leaves, and put some mousse in it—"

"The kind whose head you hang on the wall, or the kind you have for dessert?"

"The kind I use in my hair," she said tartly. "It'll make it stay the way I put it." She sprayed his hair with water and massaged in a little of the mousse. "You certainly don't have the problem the real Caesar had," she remarked idly. "He wore a wreath to hide the fact that he was going bald."

Austin made only the most minimal acknowledgment of her comment. He was lost in sensation, aware of the warmth of her body behind his as her midsection grazed his shoulders above the back of the kitchen chair. As her hands worked in his hair, the tip of her breast occasionally brushed his ear.

There were worse things to be suffered, he decided, than having Shelby Thurston weave a laurel wreath in his hair.

"If you were Socrates, what sage advice would you have for poor souls making their way through the world?" she asked.

He considered the question a moment, then said, dryly, "Don't get mixed up with women with big, sad eyes and a sob story."

Shelby whacked him with the comb playfully. "Some gratitude I get for plucking you out of an unemployment line!" She realized her blunder immediately. His entire attitude changed, and the sudden droop of his shoulders was grave.

"Did you get a raw deal at Mason Engineering?" she asked softly, then quickly added, "If you'd rather not talk about it . . ."

Austin hesitated. "I got a raw deal." He took a deep breath, exhaled raggedly. "I was in line for a vice-presidency, and Mason Junior felt threatened. He started sabotaging my projects, trying to make me look bad, arbitrarily changing specifications to show he had the authority. We wound up taking our feud to the old man."

He shook his head slowly, as though still perplexed. "I thought the old man would back me. He knew my work was sound, and Junior's . . . Issue for issue the old man always backed me when Junior came out with one of his asinine power displays. But when it came down to Junior or me, blood was thicker than water."

He shook his head again. "The old man just sat there and told me how much he valued the work I'd done for him and how sorry he was that I didn't feel I could go on working there. After I'd worked my guts out for that company." He stopped abruptly, a trifle embarrassed at having exposed his bitterness so blatantly.

"Nepotism," Shelby said thoughtfully, placing a hand on his shoulder to comfort him, "a sacred business tradition."

"You sound as though you've had some personal experience with it."

Unconsciously, she gripped his shoulder as she thought about Thurston Enterprises. "I've seen it in action."

In some inside-out, reverse discrimination sort of way, she was as affected by it as he. Wasn't that why The Shelby Agency was so important to her? The Shelby Agency, not The Thurston Agency or The Shelby Thurston Agency. Nepotism was the reason she was coercing and cajoling this perfectly divine man into wearing a toga for Caesar's Office World when she could be filling a specially created PR post at Thurston Enterprises.

There was a silence as she fiddled with the wreath. "Shake your head," she instructed finally. "Feel secure?"

Austin thrust his forefinger into the air dramatically. "A stitch in time saves nine. A rolling stone gathers no moss. Evil be to . . ." Laughing, he said, "I forgot who gets the evil."

"If that's as close as you come to ancient Greek philosophy," Shelby said, giggling, "then I think you'd better stick to the script. You're supposed to be a Roman anyway."

"Script?" Austin asked, suddenly wary.

"Don't worry about a thing," Shelby said. "There's only one line. I'll brief you when we get to the convention center."

Austin already knew Shelby well enough to get nervous when she said, "Don't worry." Heaven help me, he thought, then held out his arm as instructed so that she could slip the underarm strap of the toga in place.

Not even Shelby was prepared for the sensation her living,

breathing Caesar created at the trade show. Excited by their break in routine, the women conventioneers were in a festive mood. They flirted with Austin, some subtly, some boldly, a few almost lewdly.

Like Dr. Frankenstein, Shelby wasn't always sure how to care for her creation. As long as he stayed in the Caesar's Office World booth, he was relatively protected. But in the aisleways and the dining hall he was subjected to a constant barrage of whispered propositions, come-hither looks and wolf whistles.

A few minutes before closing, she drove her car to the service door nearest the Caesar's booth so Austin wouldn't have to walk through the crowd in the foyer. He settled into the passenger's seat, huffed indignantly and crossed his arms over his chest defiantly. The look in his eyes was menacing.

"Austin?" she said, concerned.

"I could strangle you for getting me into this, Shelby. It would be justifiable homicide."

His vehemence caught her off guard. She could understand his being tired, but he didn't have to be boorish. "You're certainly in a snit," she snapped.

Austin looked at her indignantly. "Not a jury in the world would convict me."

"I'm sure a female jury would never find you guilty of anything."

"A male jury wouldn't either if they'd been subjected . . ." Out of steam, he left the retort dangling. A charged silence stretched between them, making them both uncomfortable.

"What are you so all-fired mad about anyway?" she asked finally, unable to endure the silence any longer. "You were surrounded by adoring women today. Isn't that every man's ultimate fantasy?"

He mumbled something that sounded like, "Iga French."

"I beg your pardon," she said.

He directed a thunderous scowl in her direction. "I said, 'I got pinched.' "

"Where?" she asked incredulously.

"In the aisle, on the way to the door."

Now Shelby sniffed in exasperation. "I meant, where did they pinch you."

"Where do you think? This woman came up and said, 'Caesar was Italian, wasn't he?' and pinched me."

Shelby laughed. "No. Oh, no. That's funny."

"It's not funny, Shelby."

She was bubbling over with mirth. "It is."

"It . . ." He looked at her and burst out laughing. "It *is* funny."

Eventually their combined laughter faded into a companionable silence. Shelby shoved a cassette into the tape player while they waited for a traffic light to change. Soon lilting music reverberated through the car and Shelby felt herself relaxing after the tiring day. She hoped the music was working the same magic on Austin. His forbearance so far had impressed her, but he was, after all, only human. With the blow he'd suffered to his pride, he could decide no job was worth the humiliation and refuse to come back tomorrow.

They reached her duplex. Austin had taken the wreath out of his hair and now carried it in his hand. Shelby smiled at him when the dead bolt lock snapped open in response to the turn of her key. "I know you're anxious to get back into pants."

"You said it."

She preceded him into the house and stopped in the middle of the room, ready to help him with the unwieldy length of cloth. "As soon as we get the toga unwound the bathroom's all yours."

While he dressed, she kicked off her shoes and snuggled down in her favorite overstuffed arm chair. Minutes later Austin's voice brought her back from the verge of sleep.

"Got any Band-Aids, Shelby?"

"They're in . . . I'll find them," she called, deciding it might be easier to get them herself than try to explain where they were. "Is this for your pinched pride?" she teased, after sticking her head and shoulders into the linen closet, then reemerging with the tin of bandages.

Austin was dressed, except for one sock and his shoes. His right foot was on the rim of the tub so that the cuffs of his baggy cotton pants were hiked up over his ankle. "The *calcei* rubbed a blister."

"I'll put this on for you," she said, and then, getting a good look at the blister, added, "We should wash that before we bandage it."

"It's nothing, really. I just wanted the Band-Aid to cushion it when I put on my shoes."

"It's not nothing Austin. It's bleeding. A soapy washcloth ought to do it."

"Shelby, really."

She turned on the tap, reached into the linen closet for a fresh cloth. "You can't just put a bandage over an open wound. It'll get infected."

He was less aware of the soap stinging his heel than of Shelby's hand on the top of his foot as she dabbed the cloth over the blister with her other hand. "Does it hurt?" she asked anxiously.

"No," he said, smiling as he looked down into eyes limpid with concern. How insignificant a little physical discomfort seemed compared to the pleasure of the touch of her skin against his. "It's okay. Really."

"I'm going to put some first-aid cream on it."

He didn't protest, but watched as she foraged through the medicine chest and selected a tube of something or other.

"This won't sting," she said.

It stung. At his involuntary intake of breath, Shelby leaned forward and blew on the blister to ease the burning.

So much for fastidiousness, Austin thought. "You're putting fresh germs on it," he said, grinning.

Shelby cocked her head and stared up at him perplexedly, as though he'd deliberately insulted her and she couldn't imagine why. "They're friendly germs," she said indignantly.

"My mistake," he said, and shrugged his shoulders.

When the bandage was in place Shelby stood up. Austin slipped on his sock, took his foot from the rim of the tub, and straightened.

The room usually so familiar to Shelby suddenly seemed foreign and exotic. Austin's presence was overpowering in the narrow area between the tub and the vanity. The aura of shampoo, perfume and dusting powder that normally proclaimed the room to be uniquely hers was now mixed with the musky scent of his cologne. It had been the same in the booth at the convention center. His presence had been dominant.

"You shrank," he said, and to her puzzled look, explained. "You're shorter."

"I took off my shoes."

Swatting her hip playfully, he said, "Put them back on and I'll take you to dinner."

The intimacy stunned them both. Austin felt a sinking sensation in the pit of his stomach. Perhaps he'd inadvertently gone too far, spoiled something between them. He searched her face for a hint of what she was thinking.

Shelby wondered why she didn't feel offended or insulted that Austin had patted her on the behind. How could such a strong rapport have developed between them in the short time they'd known each other? He wanted to go to dinner. Why not? she thought. "Mind if I change clothes first?" she asked.

A softly pleated putty-colored cotton skirt and an off-white, lace-trimmed blouse were welcome replacements for her straight-skirted tailored suit, and she gratefully tossed her panty hose in the hamper and slipped on a pair of flat sandals.

She found Austin at the window in her office, watching the chattering, scratching birds gathered near the feeder she kept stocked outside. "Some environmentalists say you're not supposed to feed them, but I enjoy having them around," she said, stepping into the room. "Do you think it makes them dependent?"

"I wouldn't worry about them. They seem to be a scrappy lot." Turning, he eyed her with masculine appreciation. She looked different in her casual clothes, younger, smaller, huggable. He'd gotten a puppy for Christmas when he was a boy, and he'd carried that puppy with him everywhere, inside his jacket to keep it warm. He thought he'd like to do that to Shelby, tuck her under his arm and hold her next to him for the sheer pleasure of having her near him.

"Ready?" she asked.

"I'm starving."

They went to a small pub where the atmosphere was casual and the steaks choice. In the mellow glow of candlelight they sipped wine and talked about everything and nothing. Shelby would remember mostly that they laughed a lot, that he held her hand while they walked from the restaurant to the parking lot, and that he put his arm around her shoulders when they walked from his car to her porch.

She unlocked her door, left it ajar and turned to Austin. She could see the disappointment in his eyes as he realized she was not going to invite him in. "It's been a long day,

Austin, and tomorrow—" she began, hoping to soften the rejection.

His kiss silenced her, a gentle, titillating brush of his lips against hers. Eyes half closed, she waited breathlessly for the proper good-night kiss to come.

She looked exactly the way Austin had imagined her in his fantasies, lips full and slightly parted, willing, even asking to be kissed. In his fantasy, he gathered her in his arms and she embraced him, clung to him.

In his fantasy they were alone in a beautiful place, a private place, not on the front porch of a duplex. He ached to hold her the way he'd imagined, but she'd set the rules. Yesterday she hadn't wanted to mix business and pleasure, and tonight she hadn't invited him in.

The proper good-night kiss Shelby was waiting for never came. After several seconds of anticipation, Austin leaned forward and pressed a light kiss on her forehead. He didn't trust himself to do more than that. If he ever held her, he wasn't sure he'd be able to let her go. "See you in the morning, Shelby."

After waving goodbye and watching Austin drive off from just inside her door, Shelby slammed it shut. "See you in the morning, Shelby," she said in a high, mocking voice.

She found the folded toga in her office and the tunic in the bathroom, and tossed both of them into the washing machine, set it for a cold water delicate cycle, threw in some detergent, turned on the machine and retired to her bedroom. She would dry the emperor's clothes in the morning.

Before she saw the emperor.

"When you said lunch was provided," Austin said, "I didn't expect such lavish accommodations."

Shelby laughed. "I'm glad you've still got your sense of

humor. This really was the best I could do." They were sequestered in what amounted to a broom closet, the only secluded spot she had been able to find to get Austin away from the throng of conventioneers. Eating in the dining room the day before had been a fiasco, and Shelby had flatly refused to subject him to that exhibit-in-a-freak-show situation today.

A silence ensued as they ate roast beef sandwiches bought at a caterer's booth. Finally, Shelby laid down her sandwich and said, "You're doing a wonderful job, Austin."

" 'May I sharpen a pencil for you, compliments of Caesar's Office World?' is not a tough line."

"But you say it with such feeling," she said, biting her lip to ward off the giggle forming at the sight of the wry expression on his face.

"My mouth aches from smiling," he complained.

The giggle erupted from her throat, and she reached out to pinch his cheek playfully. "Then don't frown so. Don't you know that it takes more muscles to frown than to smile?"

"Shelby," he said, reaching up to remove her hand. As he touched her and saw the amusement twinkling in her eyes, his exasperation was transformed into a strong awareness of her as a woman. Their eyes locked in silent communication and a telling flush spread over Shelby's face, as flattering as it was revealing. Austin released her hand and she drew it away quickly.

Bracing his booted foot against the edge of a wooden crate, he tilted backward in his folding chair and said, "I don't suppose you know anything about this 'hunk' nonsense."

Guilt spread momentarily over Shelby's face then yielded to an impish, mischievous smile.

His foot slid to the floor, followed by the front legs of his chair as he sat the chair upright. "You do know something about it. Damn it, Shelby, tell me what's going on."

She shrugged, still feigning innocence, and shook her head. "I didn't have anything to do with it."

"With what?" Austin was trying hard to be angry, only to feel his irritation eroding away in the light of Shelby's amusement.

Shelby could contain her laughter no longer. It spilled into her voice as she said, "Caroline went around on her break whispering to people very confidentially that there was a hunk in booth 2245." Caroline Baxter was Mr. Caesar's administrative assistant, and she was in charge of the Caesar's booth.

Frowning, Austin said, "That explains a lot of the comments. What ever possessed her to do a thing like that? Things were crazy enough yesterday."

"Loyalty to Caesar's," Shelby said lightly. "Sex sells, you know."

Austin groaned. "I don't know how I got roped into this," he muttered, but even while he was saying it, he knew. The reason was sitting scarcely a foot away from him, brimming over with *joi de vivre,* irresistibly lovely, incredibly sexy.

Her lips were full, voluptuous as she smiled an amused smile and put her hand on his arm consolingly. "Being a sex object is difficult work, Austin," she said, "but someone has to do it. At least you're not walking a treadmill." The other hunk at the show, a weight lifter with his sun-bronzed body greased to a sheen, was demonstrating exercise equipment for office mini-gyms.

Austin refrained from commenting and took a hefty bite of his sandwich. Shelby did the same, and they finished their meal in silence. At length, Austin wadded his napkin into a ball and tossed it into a dilapidated trash can in the corner, then repeated the performance with his paper plate. Reluctantly, he dragged himself to his feet and said, "Time to sharpen some more pencils."

Shelby glanced at her watch. "You have another two or three minutes."

She was still seated, and from her low vantage point, Austin appeared larger than life, as imposing as the ancient ruler and warrior he was impersonating. His thick, sun-streaked hair swirled through the laurel leaves of the wreath that rested on his head like a crown. His strong, broad shoulders supported the weight of the heavy toga as if it were chiffon, his muscular calves tapered aristocratically into the ankle-high, open-toed *calcei.* No wonder the hunk gimmick worked. The masculine appeal of Austin Hastings and the historic charisma of Julius Caesar meshed perfectly with potent results.

He gratefully resettled into the chair next to her. Tilting his head back, he closed his eyes, exhaled heavily and said, "Four more hours." Then, opening his eyes, he glanced at Shelby. "If one more woman says, 'You can sharpen my pencil anytime,' I may make an impolite suggestion about the disposal of the pencil in question."

Shelby laughed. "Men! Now you know what women have been going through all these years. The leers, the innuendoes."

Stretching his arm across the back of her chair, Austin said, "Tell me, Ms. Thurston, are you speaking from experience?"

Involuntarily, Shelby's eyes dropped to her ample bosom, today displayed to advantage by the cowl collar of her soft silk shirt. "I was an early bloomer," she said. "Until the other girls caught up, I heard more than my share of sexist comments."

"At the risk of sounding sexist, Shelby, a woman with a

body like yours has to expect men . . ."

"And a man with your . . . assets has to expect women . . ." she said, letting her voice trail off just as he had.

Austin smiled wryly. "Perhaps two people as magnificent as we are should team up." His voice had taken on a husky quality, and Shelby felt color rising in her cheeks.

"I . . . uh, think I'd better get you back to your public," she said, consulting her watch. She stood up, then, while slipping on her suit jacket, she added lightly, "Dozens of drooling women are waiting in line to have their pencils sharpened."

He covered her hand as she reached for the doorknob, drawing her attention. "Those women outside," he said, nodding toward the convention hall, "they're just a job. But you're more than a boss."

Not sure how to answer him, Shelby stared down at their hands on the doorknob. After a few awkward seconds of hesitation she pulled the door open and hid behind a mask of crisp professionalism as they stepped into the hall.

Austin did not touch her as he followed her through the crowded aisles of the show hall, but he was constantly aware of the feminine slope of her shoulders, the scent of her perfume, the way her dark hair glistened even in the harsh lights of the hall.

With his thoughts focused on Shelby, he was largely oblivious to the reaction of the crowd around them, the gasps, sighs, giggles and flippant comments. Four hours, he was thinking. Four hours and this ridiculous Caesar business would be over. And more significantly, he would no longer be in Shelby's employ. Then he'd learn whether her objection to getting involved while they were working together was a legitimate concern or if she was just stringing him along so he would play Caesar for her client.

Austin loathed himself for doubting her. He couldn't remember when he'd found a woman as fascinating as Shelby, or when he'd needed the diversion of a fascinating woman so badly. But the suspicion—or the fear—that she was using him lingered in a corner of his mind.

Caroline greeted them effusively as they approached the Caesar's Office World booth. "I see you brought some camp followers with you."

Austin turned to discover that a number of women had fallen into step behind him and were milling about in a loose line, grinning and chattering amiably as they waited for whatever it was that Caesar the Hunk was going to do. He looked at Shelby as if to say, can you believe this? She struggled to keep a straight face and shook her head gently.

Austin squared his shoulders, turned to the first woman in line, smiled and said, "May I sharpen a pencil for you, compliments of Caesar's Office World?"

The woman nodded and giggled nervously. Shelby slapped a pencil into Austin's open hand. He jammed it into the electric pencil sharpener, and the machine's mechanical whine added to the din in the hall. Austin removed the pencil, examined the new point and, finding it acceptable, handed it to the woman. With a muted thank-you she walked away.

"May I sharpen a pencil for you, compliments of Caesar's Office World?" he asked the next woman in line, holding up his hand for a new pencil.

"Honey, any man who looks like you can sharpen my pencil any time," the woman replied as Austin's fingers closed around the pencil Shelby had put in his hand.

Austin heard Shelby's soft gasp as she stepped behind him. Her lips almost touched his ear as she whispered over his shoulder, "Remember, Caesar, your job is to be charming."

She needn't have worried. He was the soul of charm, a model of courtliness, even when the afternoon began to seem interminable and there was no break in the parade of women lined up at the booth to get a peep at the hunk in the toga. Shelby could see the fatigue in Austin's face, but his smile was unwavering.

At a quarter to five, Shelby rested her hand on his back comfortingly and whispered, "Fifteen minutes." She was ill-prepared for the look he cast in her direction as he nodded to indicate he'd heard her, and the visual exchange was so brief that she was left wondering if she'd really seen the glint of desire in his eyes or only imagined it. She inhaled deeply. Whether he meant to or not, the Caesar she'd created had a way of doing crazy things to her pulse rate.

They were almost out of pencils, so she foraged under the curtain behind the booth for a new box and emerged just in time to hear a woman tell Austin, "You can sharpen my pencils any time, Caesar." Probably because it had been a long day and she was tired of the confinement of the booth, the overworked line struck her as hilarious, and the sight of Austin's jaw clenching behind his fixed smile seemed even funnier.

Struggling to contain her laughter, she ducked behind Austin as a peculiar wheeze escaped from her throat. Pressing her forehead into his spine, she fought to maintain her composure.

"Here you go, ma'am," Austin told the customer. "Now if you should break this point, day or night, weekend or weekday, just take it to any Caesar's store, and we'll get it resharpened."

"Austin!" she wheezed, pummeling his shoulder blade with her fist.

His voice was suddenly musical as he addressed the next woman in line. "May I sharpen a pencil for you, compliments of Caesar's Office World?" He quickly added, "Don't worry about a thing, Shelby. Everything's under control. I can take the pencils out of the box by myself."

"You'll have to excuse my assistant," he told the woman. "She doesn't get out much, and she's a bit overstimulated."

"It's being in the presence of greatness," she said wryly, stepping back to her post behind the counter.

There was no more silliness. Austin greeted the last-minute stragglers with the same equanimity he'd shown all day, even though it meant working a few minutes after the booth was officially closed. He watched the last woman tuck her Caesar's Office World pencil into her already bulging plastic shopping bag and turned to find Shelby eyeing him intently.

"You're quite a man, Caesar."

His eyes swept over her face, warming as sunshine. "I'm trying to impress the boss." Then, in an abrupt change of mood, he flung his arm across her shoulders, and said, "Let's get out of here."

Shelby turned to Caroline and started to say something, but Caroline forestalled her protest by raising her hand. "You two go on. You've done all the work. The booth is my baby. I'll see that the leftover pencils get back to the warehouse."

Austin's arm remained across Shelby's shoulders as they walked through the aisles, sidestepping stray boxes and miscellaneous paraphernalia jutting from booths being dismantled. The foyer of the exhibit hall was deserted except for a few isolated clusters of lingering conventioneers and workers walking to or from the exhibit area carrying boxes or pushing dollies.

Austin slowed his pace as they approached the broom closet. "Isn't that our dining room?"

Before Shelby could question why, he had whisked her into the inelegant little room. He pushed the door shut and leaned against it.

Shelby was never sure whether what happened next actually happened slowly, or whether the intensity of it warped her perception so that Austin seemed to move in slow motion. Her first awareness was of his eyes as they studied her face, drawing her gaze, holding her in a near hypnotic state as his arms slid around her.

Trembling with anticipation, she watched his face move closer, then felt first his breath on her skin and then the fluttering touch of his lips on hers. She sighed softly, and Austin instantaneously tightened his hold on her, pulling her to him, and kissing her properly. Afterward, he raised his head slowly and hugged her against him.

Shelby nestled her cheek in the folds of the toga. "No wonder Cleopatra went to Rome to be with Caesar."

Austin stiffened and moved his hands to her shoulders, pushing her away a bit and, thrusting his face close to hers, said, "Caesar wasn't kissing you, Shelby, Austin Hastings was. I'm not Julius Caesar, and I'm not the hunk from booth 2245."

She raised her hands to caress his face, then slid her fingers up through his hair and, lifting the wreath out of it, slipped it over her wrist and onto her arm like a bracelet. Her voice was husky as she peered into his eyes. "I happen to think that Austin Hastings is quite a hunk."

She ran her fingers through his hair again, and Austin met her halfway as she stood on tiptoe to return the kiss he'd given her.

Chapter Four

"Dinner again?" Austin asked as Shelby drove to the duplex.

"How about something casual at my place?"

He cocked an eyebrow at her. "The lady cooks?"

"I said casual. The menu depends on what's in the cupboard."

"Sounds good to me," Austin said. Better than good; perfect. There was no one he wanted more to be with than Shelby, and no place he'd prefer to be with her than in her own home.

Shelby changed into pants and a baggy knit shirt and was sitting Indian-style on the sofa reading the *Sentinel* when Austin came out of the bathroom with the toga in his arms. "Do we burn this and put the ashes in an urn?" he asked.

"Mr. Caesar would go into apoplexy," Shelby said. "Just lay it on the sideboard there and I'll wash it and give it to him next time I see him. He may want to resurrect Old Julius sometime."

"Heaven forbid," Austin said, sitting down on the sofa next to her, thinking how small she looked. Her feet were bare, and her toenails were painted fire-engine red. He wondered what she would do if he flung his arms around her and pulled her onto his lap. *And made mad, passionate love to her?* he thought, grinning wickedly. He leaned forward, clamped his hand at the nape of her neck familiarly, and began to read the newspaper headlines over her shoulder. "Any big news?"

"Same old thing," she answered.

"Got a sports page there?"

"Take it all," she said, handing him the entire paper. "I'm going to check out the pantry."

The sports section was a poor replacement for her company. After skimming the headlines, he tossed the paper aside and walked to the kitchen. Shelby was setting the dials on the microwave, and an assortment of cans and cannisters cluttered the work counter. He picked up one of the cans and read the label: tomato paste. "What's the verdict?" he asked.

"How do you feel about spaghetti?"

"Personally or politically?"

Satisfied with the settings on the computerized controls, Shelby pressed the button that put the microwave into action, then turned to Austin. "We're having it for dinner. Is that personal or political?"

"I like spaghetti," he said, chuckling.

"Great. The chopping board's in that drawer, and the knives are in the holder in front of you. The onion is already washed. Finely chopped, if you please."

"Yes, ma'am," he said, looking over the knives in the wooden holder.

Shelby took a bowl and measuring cup from the cupboard and turned on the tap. Leaving it running, she stepped behind Austin, putting her hand on his shoulder as she stood on tiptoe to look over him at the collection of supplies she'd gathered. "Would you hand me the yeast, please? I can't reach it."

He held up the foil envelope. "Is this it?"

Nodding, she took it. "Thanks."

"Are you making homemade noodles?"

She chuckled. "Not with yeast! This is for the bread sticks." Making a face, she said, "Whew, that onion's strong."

Rubbing his eyelids with the back of his hand, Austin agreed. "Very."

"Don't rub your eyes like that. It just makes it worse." She ran a clean cloth under the tap, wrung it out, pressed it against his eyelids gently. "Better?"

"Um-hm."

"Good," Shelby said with a sniff, "because now my eyes are burning."

Each squinted at the other, then they both burst into laughter. Putting his arm across her shoulders, Austin led her to the far side of the kitchen. Their laughter slowly diminished, fading into something different, something warm and wonderful between them. As he hugged her, she slipped her arms around his waist, snuggled close to him and sighed against his shoulder. Then Shelby tilted her head back, eager for his kiss, and his lips grazed her forehead.

The spontaneity of the kiss made it special. No pretenses or apprehensions marred the magic of being embraced by his strong arms and tenderly caressed by his gentle hands. Shelby gave herself up to the feelings his touch evoked. She was a woman, voluptuous and desirable; he was a man, warm and strong, who desired her. Yet his touch was gentle. It was to his tenderness she responded most ardently, because the tenderness made it a private, personal thing. His lips were gentle, then demanding. Shelby was thrilled.

He held her after he'd kissed her and said huskily, "I like the way you make spaghetti."

She chuckled against his chest. "I like the way you chop onions."

Reluctantly they returned to the tasks at hand.

Once the onions were sauteed and the sauce was stirred together and left to simmer, Austin leaned against the counter and watched Shelby knead the dough for the bread sticks. He liked watching her, appreciating her physical perfection as he would that of a sleek thoroughbred. She was full of surprises. "Where did you learn to make bread?" he asked.

"Hanging around the kitchen when I was a kid." She faced him. "Bread's not difficult, really. It just takes time. Bread sticks don't even take much of that."

"What now?" he asked as she slid the ball of dough into the bowl she'd greased, turned it, and covered it with a cotton sack dishcloth.

"This is the tough part," she said, grinning impishly. Then she whispered conspiratorially, "We go relax while the yeast works."

"So what are you going to do now that you're not Julius Caesar anymore?" she asked, when they had settled side by side on the sofa.

He shrugged. "Find a job." He shook his head. "I'm . . . I still can't believe it, you know. I say that I'm going to go out and find a job, but it hasn't even soaked in yet that I don't still have a job. I left Mason's on Thursday, I was with you yesterday and today, tomorrow's Sunday. It's incomprehensible to me that Monday will come and I won't have a job to go to."

Shelby ached with the pain he was feeling. He was so big and strong, yet so vulnerable. He'd been betrayed and he was hurting inside. She reached out, put her hand over his and squeezed it. "You'll get another job."

He forced a smile. "I know. It's just . . . it happened so fast. I haven't had time to think about it. I'm not sure I know where to start."

"I'll bet you've already started."

His smile had faded and been replaced by a grim stoicism. "I have an appointment with a headhunter Monday afternoon."

Shelby scooted closer to him, slipped her right arm across

his chest and up to his shoulder. "Bet you a kiss you've either got a suit hanging in a cleaning bag in your closet or you've got a suit at the cleaners ready to be picked up before your interview."

This earned a wry grin. It was a bet he didn't mind losing. "I dropped off my best suit and my best tie on the way to the unemployment office Thursday. I was planning on picking them up Monday morning."

"See. You're not sitting staring into space wondering what to do. You're already working on getting another job."

How intriguing her eyes were, so big and brown and bright. Austin could see his face reflected in them as he looked at her. He wanted to tell her how much it meant to him that she had confidence in him when his own confidence was waning, but he wasn't sure how. "Aren't you going to collect on your bet?" he asked.

"I'm going to put the kiss I won in my pocket for safe-keeping," she said, smiling enigmatically.

"You can't put a kiss in your pocket."

"Sure I can. It'll fit right next to my Brownie smile."

"Your what smile?"

"Obviously you were never a Brownie Girl Scout," she said haughtily.

He chuckled, genuinely amused. "No. I wasn't."

"Brownies keep a smile in their pockets, and I still have mine," she said. "And now I have the kiss, too, just in case I need it."

"You're incredible. Did you know that?"

Tilting her head back vampishly, she regarded him through lowered eyelids. "Are you referring to the amazing self-control that enables me to resist kissing you?"

He brushed a strand of hair from her forehead. "No, Shelby. Why would you think you have to hoard away one of my kisses when all you'd have to do is look at me the way you're looking at me now and you could have all the kisses you want?"

"You never know. You might discover that I have some irritating habit that drives you mad."

"If you drive me mad, it won't be because of an irritating habit." His voice was suddenly husky. He cradled her face in his hands, leaned forward and kissed her gently on the lips. "I wouldn't even get irritated at you for eating crackers in bed."

Shelby tensed. Damn it, why was it every time she met a man she liked, sex had to become an issue right away? Austin's casual, suggestive comment was only the beginning. Soon he would be pressuring her to go to bed with him. She touched the rugged beauty of his face with her fingertips, and sadness that it soon would be over stabbed through her. She would refuse to sleep with him. She just wasn't ready for that type of involvement, and he would probably lose interest in her before she became ready. It was all too familiar a cycle, but for Shelby it would never work. She simply was not the kind of woman who could rush into a physical relationship with a man.

Austin sensed her withdrawal. A shadow of sadness crept into her eyes as her fingers caressed his cheek. Taking her hand in his, he kissed the inside of her palm, then released it. She looked at the backs of her fingers, nervously nudged at a cuticle with the thumb of her other hand, then dropped both hands into her lap as she leaned against the back of the sofa.

Austin frowned, suddenly angry at himself. His careless remark had destroyed something between them, something he could sense but not define, something that allowed them to be comfortable in each other's company. "So how did you come to start your own business?" he asked, anxious to put her at her ease again.

Glad that he had changed the subject, Shelby told him

about majoring in public relations in college, about her three years spent progressing from editorial assistant and receptionist to assistant account representative, about her realization that she was doing a lot of work for very little credit and even less money. "I decided to try opening my own agency," she said. "It's been touch and go, but business is picking up. I'm relying heavily on Mr. Caesar for some referrals. He deals with some heavyweights from a number of businesses at his computer center in the I-4 store."

He followed her to the kitchen and watched as she stirred the spaghetti sauce. Then he became involved in pinching circles of dough and rolling them between his hands to form the bread sticks. Shelby assigned him the job of painting the bread sticks with beaten egg and sprinkling them with sesame seeds while she washed lettuce for the salad.

"Are you sure this is how bakeries do it?" he asked, eyeing the slimy eggs on the pastry brush skeptically.

"It makes them crisp on the outside," she assured him. Later, when he'd eaten about a dozen of the finished product and was dipping still another into soft butter, she asked, "Believe me now about the eggs?"

"I believe. Woman, you are one hell of a cook." His capacity for spaghetti had proven to be only slightly less prodigious than his capacity for bread sticks.

"Keep flattering the cook that way and you might get invited back."

"I'll count on it," he said. Her cooking was not all he admired about her. The expression in his eyes as he looked at her drew her attention and held it. An awareness crackled between them, and Shelby felt a warmth spreading inside her. Reaching over to take her hand in his, he stood up, and she rose and stepped into the welcoming circle of his arms.

For a while, nothing mattered beyond the reach of those

arms, nothing existed except for his hard body against hers and the feel of his strong arms around her. He kissed her, then held her tight, cuddling her against him. But he didn't slip his hand into her blouse and touch those full, ripe breasts he longed to touch. He didn't try to seduce her into bed. He would have done that on Thursday if she hadn't stopped him from kissing her. On Thursday, he could have taken her to bed and walked away with no regrets when the fireworks were spent. But it was no longer Thursday. It was Saturday, and the intervening hours spent with Shelby had been significant ones. He could no longer separate his feelings into little compartments labeled sexual desire, respect, and affection. Nothing between them was casual, not even the rapport that made them so comfortable with each other. An affair wouldn't be casual, either, even if Shelby were willing to go to bed with him, which, judging from her reaction to his crackers-in-bed remark, she wasn't.

So instead of trying to seduce her, he put his arm across her shoulders, thanked her for the dinner and offered to help with the dishes. Then they watched a movie Shelby had recorded but never found time to watch. It turned out to be mediocre, a clumsy comedy more worthy of groans than laughs. It didn't matter. Austin and Shelby groaned *and* laughed, mimicking the actors, delivering corny lines and predicting upcoming punch lines. At the end of the movie, the hero and heroine were clutched in an embrace.

"Now that," Austin said, "is the most intelligent thing that boob has done during the entire movie."

Shelby wasn't sure whether to laugh or swoon as he grasped her and began administering an exaggerated stage kiss, but her confusion soon dissipated when she found herself trapped under his body, and his tongue swept over her bottom lip.

Her eyes opened wide, and she found Austin's eyes were also open, registering as much surprise as she was feeling. Austin's breath was warm and moist against her cheek as he stared down at her. For an immeasurable expanse of time, they were totally motionless, and then slowly, so slowly that she thought she might not be able to bear the waiting, his face lowered over hers and his lips claimed hers. The kiss was sweet, passionate, demanding, giving: a rare, exquisite sharing of pleasure, emotion, affection and adoration.

Shelby made a sound that was half sigh, half gasp as Austin pulled away from her.

"I think I'd better go now," he said, and then, searching her face, added hopefully, "unless you want me to stay."

Chapter Five

It's too soon, Shelby thought, wishing her pulse weren't racing, that her breasts weren't still tingling in response to the pressure of his chest, that she wasn't so intimately aware of his physical readiness to make love and the answering warmth spreading through her own body.

For a moment she vacillated, torn between logic and impulse but finally she answered, "I think it's time for you to go."

With a whispered, "Good night," and a brief brush of his lips over hers, he left. Shelby walked with him to the door and, after engaging the lock, leaned against the door, closed her eyes and sighed, imagining Austin's face and remembering the feel of his body against hers.

Strangely, joyously exhilarated, she felt she should be dancing or singing or running barefoot across a sunlit meadow. What a man! What a perfectly divine hunk of masculinity! How could a man look like that and have his sense of humor? And he'd left, accepted her judgment. He hadn't pressured her, hadn't made it ugly. If he had argued with her about leaving, the special quality of the evening would have been lost as suddenly and surely as the air from a punctured balloon.

In the bedroom, she reached for her favorite knit dorm shirt, then impulsively lifted a satin gown from her drawer instead. The cloth was cool and slick as it settled over her bare skin, and she soothed the dolman sleeve of the shirt, letting her hand rest on her arm for a few seconds. On her way to the bathroom, she caught sight of her reflection in the antique cheval glass. Her skin appeared smooth through the lace appliques that swirled from one shoulder to the top of the opposite breast, and the scarlet satin emphasized the flush that lingered on her cheeks.

Gingerly, she reached up to touch the spot of color with her fingertips, wondering what Austin would think if he could see her in the satin gown, *wishing* Austin could see her, because she knew the color was flattering and she wanted him to think her beautiful.

"Beautiful?" she said aloud, with a bit of self-deprecation. Assuming a sensual pose, chest out, chin up, head tilted in front of the cheval glass, she wondered if the dreamy-eyed woman reflected there could possibly be Shelby Thurston.

Realizing what she was doing, she stared for a moment at the stranger she'd become, then frowned and turned away from the cheval glass. She became aware of a tightness in her chest, a fear. It was happening too fast. She was getting too deeply involved, too quickly, and leaving herself vulnerable. She would not put herself in a position of getting hurt. No man, not even a hunk like Austin Hastings, was going to get close enough to her to hurt her until she could trust him. She had learned through personal experience that fools who rushed into affairs of the heart got hurt, and she wasn't going to play the fool for any man ever again. Her emotional scars went too deep for her to make the same mistake twice.

"Would you like a table now, sir, or do you want to wait for your party in the bar?"

Austin looked at the nearly full dining room and the cluster of diners that had come in during the five minutes he'd been waiting in line to tell the hostess how many were in his party. If he waited much longer and Shelby was delayed, it could be an hour or more before they'd get a table.

"Table for two," he told the hostess. "Nonsmoking."

She led him to a small table next to the window. The cafe curtains covered the glass only halfway up so that he could see the bank of shrubs against the building and, beyond the greenery, the parking lot and highway.

The waitress came, and Austin ordered a drink, then told her he was waiting on someone and would order his meal later. The cold drink relieved his dry throat. It was a sunny, warm day with not a trace of the usual afternoon showers to cool it off, and the exhaustive interview with the placement consultant had left him parched.

The gleam of Shelby's metallic blue Daytona Shelby Z caught his eye as she drove into a parking slot, and he watched her walk toward the restaurant. She was wearing a black-and-white vertically striped dress with a chic red blazer over it. Her hair was pulled back away from her face on the sides, and hung in loose waves to her shoulders. She had chosen lipstick the same bright red of the blazer, and the contrast between her dark hair and creamy skin seemed a striking, coordinated extension of the black-and-white theme.

As always, he was impressed by her aplomb, by the sureness of her step and her comfortable sense of herself. Mostly, though, he was awed by her—not just her beauty and the way she presented herself, but by the knowledge that she was here, at this specific place and time, to be in his company. When she was with him, she had a way of bringing him out of himself, temporarily overpowering the sense of disenfranchisement that had been plaguing him since he'd left the Mason Engineering office with the taste of bile in his mouth and a bitterness in his heart.

It took a few minutes for Shelby to work her way through

the line at the hostess station. Austin stood up as she approached the table. He was quite impressive in his dark suit. *A man for all ages,* Shelby thought as he helped her slide her chair under the table. *Toga to three-piece.*

"How was your meeting?" he asked.

She flashed him a wide, enthusiastic smile as she accepted the tall menu the waitress handed her. "I've got a new client, thanks to a referral from Mr. Caesar. He must be pleased with the way the trade show went. How about your interview? Was it productive?"

"Fair-to-middling," Austin answered. "They're familiar with my work and reputation. They've approached me a couple of times when they had client companies looking for someone in my field, and they say they think they can place me within a couple of months. It's just a matter of the right position coming open."

"There's a big, 'but,' coming, I can tell," Shelby said. Her broad smile had faded into a pleasant, interested expression.

"My résumé has to be reworked immediately," he said sheepishly. Her perception was incredibly astute. No secrets could be kept from Shelby Thurston. "It hasn't been updated since I went to work for Mason." He frowned, and imitated the placement consultant's superior attitude. "It's stale."

"You could always try wrapping it in a damp paper towel and putting it in the microwave," Shelby quipped.

Austin looked at her as though she'd lost her senses. She shrugged. "It works with stale bread."

"I think I'll try penciling in a few updates and dropping it by a secretarial service."

"You don't type?"

"Only with my elbows," he replied. "And I don't own a typewriter."

She smiled at him smugly. "I have a computer with a word

processing program and a very sophisticated printer."

"I couldn't ask—"

"Sure you can. You saved my bacon playing Caesar. I can return the favor."

He was still undecided. She reached across the table to cover his hand with hers, and leaned forward slightly. "I know résumés, Austin. I worked in a personnel office a couple of summers, and I saw lots of them. Besides that, I'm a PR specialist. I know how to present information in a positive way."

Austin stared at her face, overwhelmed by her energy, her enthusiasm, the vibrant sparkle in her eyes. "What kind of vitamins do you take?" he asked lightly.

"Vitamins?"

He waved his hand in the air. "Just a rhetorical question."

"You're changing the subject," she said. "We can work on your résumé tonight if you don't have any plans."

"Okay . . . if I can hire you."

"Hire me?"

"Yes. You're a PR consultant. I'll commission you to do my résumé."

"My fees are pretty stiff," she challenged.

He wasn't put off. "Your work is worth it, isn't it?"

"Yes, but . . ."

But I'm a charity case, he thought bitterly, his pride smarting. He said, harshly, "I'm unemployed, Shelby, not destitute. It makes sense for me to invest in a solid résumé. I was going to pay the secretarial service, you know."

She smiled prettily and said, "Not what I'm going to charge you."

"It's tax deductible," he answered dryly.

After dinner they went to the duplex to work on the résumé. Shelby changed into jeans and a shirt while Austin went over his current version, scribbling notes in the margins. He'd taken off his suit coat and loosened his tie and appeared very comfortable as he worked at her desk. He looked up and smiled as she entered the room. "Hope you can read my handwriting."

"Probably not," she said, stepping behind him and reading over his shoulder. "Engineers rank right up there with doctors when it comes to penmanship. I was counting on you sticking around in case I had any questions."

Swiveling the chair around unexpectedly, he grabbed her wrist and pulled her into his lap and kissed her neck. "You'll have to kick me out to get rid of me."

Giggling, Shelby said, "Mr. Hastings, please. That's not part of the service."

"I thought you believed in keeping your clients happy."

She slipped her arms around his neck and kissed him full on the lips, then whispered, "Happy now, Mr. Hastings?"

With her firm, round hips pressing into his thighs, and her magnificent breasts against his chest, did she really have to ask? He hugged her, produced a sound that was equal parts sigh, groan and sensual growl, and said, "I'm in heaven, woman."

"Good," she said, picking up the paper in front of him. "Now we can tend to business." Concentrating on the dry details of the résumé was not as easy for Shelby as she pretended, but she managed to force herself to skim the information. "What's this?" she asked. "Were you nominated for Central Florida Outstanding Young Engineer this year or last year?"

"Both."

"Two years in a row?" she asked to be sure she understood him correctly. He nodded. "How many do they nominate?" she asked.

"Four."

"That's pretty impressive, to have been nominated two years in a row."

He shrugged. "It's not unusual to be nominated several times."

"Why didn't you win?" she said, softening the question by tracing her forefinger around his ear.

Only Shelby could ask something like that and not be offensive, Austin thought. Laughing softly, he said, "I'm too young."

"Too young to be Young Engineer of the Year?"

"The Engineering Society of Central Florida likes its young engineers to be closer to forty than to thirty."

"So a nomination means as much as the award."

"You hang the award on your office wall. The nomination looks good on a résumé. I'm not sure either of them means anything."

She kissed him on the nose. "You'll win it eventually."

That wasn't likely after what the headhunter had told him today, Austin thought. The counselor had advised him to relocate, get a fresh start after the sour experience with Mason, go outside the tight-knit engineering community in Central Florida. His reputation was solid, his work was impressive, but as long as he stayed in Central Florida, the brouhaha at Mason Engineering would hang around his neck like an albatross. The headhunter was planning on sending résumés to affiliated offices throughout Florida and in selected "hot spots" where industry was booming. While Austin hated the thought of ripping up the roots he'd put down over the past five years, he accepted the logic in the counselor's suggestion. Tampa, Miami, Tallahassee, Pensacola, he could end up in any corner of the state or maybe even out of state.

Crazy as it seemed, his biggest regret when he thought of leaving Orlando was sitting in his lap at the moment. He'd known her less than a week, but Austin felt a little guilty over not mentioning the relocation to Shelby. Maybe he was selfish, but something unique was happening between them and he didn't want to chance interrupting it; he was curious to see where it was leading. It was all speculation at this point, anyway. *When* he got an offer, and *if* he decided to take it, *then* he'd worry about telling Shelby. In the meantime, he'd just keep hoping some dynamic firm in Tampa would discover they needed a crackerjack engineer. Tampa would get him far enough away from Orlando, but within easy weekend commuting distance.

Pain penetrated his consciousness. Shelby was knocking on his head with her fist. Flinching, he said, "Mercy, woman! What gives?"

"Just seeing if anyone's at home," she said. "I think you were off on some desert island with a beautiful blonde."

He hugged her and kissed her on the cheek. "You're the only woman I'd want to be on a desert island with."

"Don't sweet talk me, Hastings. I've got work to do, and I can't do it while there's more than one person in this chair."

"Are you kicking me out?"

"Only as far as the living room so I can concentrate on my typing."

He whispered into her ear, "Do I distract you?"

"Yes. You also raise my knees too high to fit under the desk."

"Let's forget the résumé," he said, nibbling at the tender flesh under her ear.

The tiny kisses were doing crazy things to her pulse rate. "Oh, no!" she said, sliding his arms from around her and standing up. "You hired a seasoned pro to revise your résumé, and you're going to get quality work."

A sadness knifed through Austin when she stood up. He

was very aware that he'd lost something precious, something he didn't want to lose. He stood up. "Let me make love to you," he said abruptly, as surprised by the sudden appeal as Shelby.

Watching the emotions flash in her limpid brown eyes he steeled himself for the rejection he could tell was coming.

She stepped forward, slipped her arms around his waist, pressed her cheek against his chest and spoke so softly that he felt her words as much as heard them. "I like you, Austin."

"There's a big but coming—I can tell," he said. Feeling her tension, he stroked her hair and lied softly, "It's okay." But it wasn't okay. He wanted her, needed her, needed to touch her, to possess her. "We'll wait until you're ready." That, at least, wasn't a lie; it was an inevitable, unavoidable truth.

Neither of them missed the assumption in the statement that eventually they would be together.

And neither of them questioned it.

Chapter Six

Ramon Caesar's office was filled with the latest in technological office supplies. Only the untidy sprawl of papers nestled among the intercoms, hi-tech organizers, dictation machines and computer components indicated a human influence in the room. Mr. Caesar rose from his oak-and-leather chair and reached across the desk top to shake hands when Shelby entered. "I'm glad you were able to stop in," he said.

Their agreement had been that he would mail Austin's check to her, but his secretary had called and informed Shelby that Mr. Caesar would like to see her, and suggested she pick up the check in person. Shelby appeared the epitome of a confident, efficient businesswoman in her tailored navy suit, but she was vaguely apprehensive over being summoned to Mr. Caesar's office.

"I wanted to tell you personally how pleased I was with the trade show," he said, and Shelby relaxed. She had hoped that was why she'd been summoned. "It's a little early for solid results, but we've had a surge in sales this week, and the only thing I can attribute it to is the trade show. We've been going to that show for seven years, and we've offered the same discount incentives every year, but this is the first time we've seen this kind of response. The obvious conclusion is that your living Caesar made people notice our booth."

"The crowd certainly seemed attentive."

"The comments have all been positive," he continued. "Caroline tells me your Caesar created quite a sensation. It seems you were right all along about a gimmick, Shelby," he said, leaning his head against the back of the chair.

"Sometimes gimmicks click, and sometimes they don't," she said humbly, knowing Mr. Caesar appreciated humility in his hired help. "Caesar clicked."

"Only because you bullied me into having him there in the first place."

Humility was one thing; groveling was another. She was not going to deny that she'd fought for her idea, and he'd resisted every inch of the way. She regarded him silently with a pleasant expression on her face and waited for him to continue.

"I gave you a hard time," he said. "I'm sorry. Obviously you know a lot more about public relations than I do."

"You had the acumen to hire a professional."

Mr. Caesar smiled shrewdly. "You're a smart woman, Shelby. You know how to flatter without kowtowing." He picked up an envelope with the Caesar's Office World logo in the upper left corner, and held it out to her. "The check for your living Caesar." Shelby took it and slid it into her portfolio without looking at it.

"You'll find two checks," Mr. Caesar said. "The second one is a little irritation bonus for you for putting up with me."

"Mr. Caesar . . ." she said, surprised.

"I insist," he said firmly. "I plan to be retaining your services for some time, and I like to keep my people—my good people—happy."

"Well, thank you."

"Don't thank me too quickly," he said. "I plan to keep you pretty busy. Starting this Saturday."

"Saturday?"

"There's a pre-semester orientation weekend at the college in Gainesville, and I've hired a vendor's booth for Saturday. We have a store a few blocks from campus, and we rely heavily on the student trade. I got to thinking that your Caesar might be quite a hit with the students." He cleared his throat significantly. "Especially the coeds."

Shelby laughed. So Caroline had told him about the hunk in booth 2245. And then she remembered Austin. Oh, Lord, how would she ever coerce Austin into wearing that toga again, especially around a passel of giddy coeds? No way in God's green earth, that's how.

Mr. Caesar read her change of mood. "You don't have a prior commitment on Saturday, do you?" he asked, in a tone of voice that indicated the only prior commitment suitable would be the funeral of a family member. Anything else would be too frivolous.

"No, sir," she said. "It's just . . . I hope I can get a Caesar by then."

"Oh, we must have the same Caesar. I understand he was superb." His eyes narrowed. "Try, Shelby."

"I'll do what I can," she said.

"I knew I could count on you. I told Stewart Hargrove as much Sunday at golf, and that was before I saw any sales figures."

"I wanted to thank you for the referral," she said. "I met with Mr. Hargrove, and we have a contract pending."

"Stewart's in good hands." He paused and looked down at his desk blotter thoughtfully. "Would it help your negotiations any if we raised Caesar's pay, say—" he shrugged "—twenty-five dollars. Plus mileage to Gainesville?"

"I don't know," she said. "I'll give it a try." She doubted the money would make any difference to Austin, but she wasn't going to foul up a pay raise for him. Now all she had to do was find a way to persuade him to play Caesar again.

She stewed over the dilemma all the way home. There

must be some way to convince Austin to do it. Open, honest appeal had worked once, but this time was different.

On the way home she stopped at the supermarket and bought steaks, fresh asparagus, romaine lettuce, blue cheese, a bottle of wine, a bouquet of cut flowers, and an ample supply of candles to go in her cut crystal candleholders. She'd need all the heavy artillery she could get. Austin was coming over to pick up his check, and she had called from the pay phone in Mr. Caesar's office building to invite him for dinner.

"Maybe I should have dressed," Austin said when he saw the candle-flanked flowers and the wineglasses on the table.

"Don't be silly. We're grilling." She kissed him on the cheek. "You look fine. Just *fine,*" she said, stretching out the word for emphasis. He was wearing his cotton baggies again, with a khaki-colored tank top. "Do you lift weights or what?" she asked, tracing a forefinger over his generous biceps.

"I work out at the gym a couple of times a week."

"It works."

He reached out, put his arm around her waist and pulled her to him. "The better to hold you with," he said, and kissed her.

Shelby formed the bread sticks she'd mixed earlier and popped them in the oven while Austin tended the steaks. At the last minute, while Austin worked the corkscrew into the bottle cork, Shelby took the *coup de gras* from the refrigerator and broke an egg over the salad. Catching on, Austin threw back his head and laughed. "It's not?"

"It is," she said. "Caesar salad. Minus the anchovies."

"I love Caesar salad," he said, leaning over to kiss the tip of her nose. "Without anchovies." The cork came out of the bottle with a minimal pop and he poured the wine.

Shelby lifted her glass for a toast. The candle on her side of the table shone through the amber liquid. "To paychecks," she said.

Austin had forgotten all about the paycheck the moment he'd seen the elegant table Shelby had set. He'd forgotten why he was there, except to be near Shelby. Foremost in his mind was the fact that he wanted her, and that, perhaps, she'd changed her mind about making love with him and flowers and candlelight was her way of telling him. If so, he was going to let her tell him in her own way, wait for the subtlety of the seduction that would make it even more special.

If he didn't die of frustration first. She was incredibly alluring in those shorts she was wearing. He'd never really paid a lot of attention to her legs before, but they were great legs, long and lean, with exquisitely curved calves and slender ankles. Seeing her bare thighs without being able to touch them was an exquisite torture.

When they had finished with their steaks, Shelby cleared the dinner plates from the table and brought out parfait glasses filled with a light chocolate mousse.

"This isn't left over from that can of stuff you used on my hair, is it?" Austin said.

"No," she said. "This is strictly for the palate. Carryout from a deli-bakery."

He looked at her from over her glass. "You realize I'll have to work out *three* times next week after this."

"You're not alone. I may wear out my aerobics video." When they were finished, she refused to let him help with the dishes, insisting there were very few of them, and she would do them later. They refilled their wineglasses and carried them to the living room and placed them on the gold-etched lacquer coasters on the coffee table in front of the sofa. "Have a seat," Shelby said. "I'll get your check."

The frustration kept building in Austin. It was wearing on

his nerves. He wanted to scream at her that the check was not important, that he desperately needed to hold her. She left the room, returned carrying an envelope, which she laid on the coffee table. "Mr. Caesar was thrilled with the reports on the show. His sales have already picked up."

His mumbled "Good" was decidedly unenthusiastic.

"I even got a bonus," she said, settling next to him, close enough for him to smell her perfume. She laughed nervously. "If this keeps up, The Shelby Agency might even show a profit this quarter."

He risked putting his hand on her knee. "I'm glad it worked out for you." In his mind, he languidly slid his hand up her thigh and Shelby sighed. Shelby sighed a lot in his day-dreams, always in ecstasy.

She said his name, but without a sigh, most decidedly without a sigh. It was the tone of voice used by someone bringing up an unpleasant subject. A knot of apprehension formed in his gut. What if he had misread her? What if she'd brought him over and softened him up to tell him she didn't want him around anymore? The prospect knifed through his chest, a combination of fear and pain.

"What is it?" he asked, trying to keep the panic out of his voice.

She took a deep breath, like a child about to confess to some terrible deed. "Mr. Caesar was so pleased that he wants you at another show this weekend."

Austin was numb. He didn't know how he felt. He didn't even know how he was supposed to feel. Relieved? Angry? Amused? No, not amused. Definitely not amused. Exploited, that was how he felt, and manipulated, and devastatingly disappointed.

"So that's what this romantic little dinner was all about," he said coldly.

"No!" she said, and then admitted, "Well, yes. I mean, I enjoy being with you. But I didn't know how to tell you . . . to ask you . . ."

"And it never occurred to you just to come out and say, 'Austin, Mr. Caesar wants you to go to another show next weekend. Will you?' "

She sniffed, her exasperation obvious. "Of course it did. But I was afraid you'd say no."

"You knew I'd say no!" he said irritably. "So you decided to soften me up with a romantic little evening, ply me with wine, seduce me with bread sticks?"

Shelby couldn't help it. It struck her as funny. He was so furious and so serious and so filled with righteous indignation. She chuckled. "It never once occurred to me to seduce you with bread sticks."

"Life is one big joke to you, isn't it, Shelby?"

"No, Austin. Really. I was just trying to be . . . tactful."

"Tactful?" he parroted incredulously. He threw back his head and laughed. "Lady, you are certifiable."

"Oh, Austin, please don't be angry at me," she said. "I . . . Mr. Caesar is my first major client, and he was so pleased, and I want to keep pleasing him, and I couldn't possibly find a Caesar like you between now and Saturday. I don't think I could *ever* find a Caesar as good as you are."

She was not crying, but her eyes were bright with tears. He sighed in defeat. His shoulders drooped. "Damn it, Shelby."

She capped a hand over the bicep nearest her. "We'd be together all day again." Her other hand slid over his ribs, and her voice took on a husky quality. "It wasn't all that awful."

He tried to ignore the softness of her skin on his arm, the stirring warmth of her hand on his ribs. "*You* weren't wearing a toga," he growled. "*You* didn't get pinched."

"I won't leave you unprotected for a moment," she said.

"If anyone tries to pinch you I . . . I'll flatten them with a right cross."

Despite himself, Austin chuckled. "I believe you would."

"I do have a right cross," she said. "I used to box with my brothers. They had a punching bag, and I practiced all one summer."

"I believe that, too."

Her face, hope written in every feature, was inches from his, and her eyes pleaded with him silently. "Will you do it, Austin?"

He flung his arms around her in full surrender. "Hell, yes, Shelby. I'll do it." Tiny kisses of joy rained all over his face. "Just promise me one thing."

"Anything," she said from the vicinity of the small cleft in his chin.

"Don't ever ask me to do anything illegal for you. I could wind up in the electric chair."

She giggled. "You're so silly, Austin. I would never do anything illegal!"

No, he thought, tightening his arms around her, his lips instinctively finding hers. *But you sure don't play by the rules, lady.*

At the moment he didn't care.

Everything they would need to transform Austin into Caesar was packed in Shelby's tote bag along with a spare pair of jeans and a shirt for Shelby to wear home. By the end of the day, she would be raring to get out of her business clothes and relieved to trade her high-heeled pumps for sandals. She'd packed on Friday night because they were leaving early Saturday in order to get to Gainesville on time, and morning was not the time of day when Shelby functioned most efficiently.

The alarm clock rang at six-fifteen, and Shelby dragged herself out of bed after only one ten-minute snooze, but she was still putting the finishing touches on her makeup when Austin rang the doorbell at seventeen minutes to seven. "You're early," she greeted him.

Austin looked at his watch. "A whole two minutes," he said, stepping inside.

"I'm not ready," she said, making it sound slightly accusatory. "Make yourself at home. There's coffee in the coffee maker."

He watched as she scurried away in a dither, her stockinged feet padding noiselessly on the carpet. "Good morning to you, too," he said under his breath, and, after taking a mug from the cabinet, poured himself a cup of coffee. It was strong as battery acid. How could a woman who could cook the way Shelby cooked consistently abuse good ground coffee?

Austin sat down at the table and thought how lonely the normally cozy kitchen seemed without Shelby in it. He sipped the terrible coffee and wondered morosely what he was doing here and why he was on his way to make a fool of himself. When he was with Shelby, it was easy to remember that she needed him, and why it was important to help her. It was only when she wasn't close enough to cloud his thinking that the feeling of being exploited crept into his mind. She was using him, and he was malleable as moist clay under her influence.

A light rapping at the back door drew him out of his thoughts. He opened the door to a woman in a white nurse's uniform, complete with a cap. A plastic name tag identified her as Laura Rigg, R.N. He regarded her curiously, while she stared at him as though an alien from outer space had answered the door.

"I'm Laura. I live next door," she said. Austin nodded. "I was on my way to work, and I thought I heard Shelby up, and . . . *Is* Shelby here?"

"She's putting on her makeup," Austin said. "I'll call her."

"Oh, no. Don't disturb her. I'm late as it is." She handed him a slip of paper. "Please give her this for me, and tell her I'm sorry it's late, and that it's the usual story."

"Are you sure you don't want me to get Shelby?" he asked.

Laura, who had already turned away, looked back over her shoulder. "I'm sure. I'm running late. I'm supposed to go on duty at seven, and I'm not going to make it unless I hit the lights right."

Curious, Austin looked at the paper in his hand. It was a check for several hundred dollars made out to Shelby. On the memo line the notation was: rent/August.

Austin stared at it. The only thing Laura could possibly be renting from Shelby for this amount of money was the other half of the duplex, which meant Shelby *owned* the duplex he'd assumed she rented. But that didn't make sense at all. She was twenty-four years old, and she'd left a mediocre job to go into business for herself. Winter Park was an expensive place. How could a struggling entrepreneur get a mortgage on a duplex like this? He'd wondered how she even managed the payments on her car.

She walked in, all pert and perfect in a simple but elegant sheath, carrying a hanging clothes bag over her shoulder. He suddenly wondered if the thick chain necklace and ornate pendant that reached almost to her cleavage were solid gold. "I thought I heard voices," she said.

"A woman named Laura stopped by."

"From next door?" she asked casually.

"She wanted me to give you this. Said to tell you it was the usual story."

Shelby took the check, carried it into her office, and tucked it into her portfolio without looking at it. "Poor Laura. She's always late, but I try not to say anything. She always brings over a check sooner or later. She's divorced, and her ex-husband never sends his child support in time."

She tugged the shoulder strap of her tote bag over her shoulder. "Who's driv—?" Something about Austin's hostile stance, the grim set of his jaw stopped her in mid-sentence. "Is something wrong?"

"The figures," he said. "They don't add up."

"What on earth are you talking about?" she asked impatiently. The tote bag was getting heavy, and it was awkward holding both her portfolio and the garment bag. Why didn't Austin offer to carry something? He was usually so considerate.

"You *own* this building," he said, still not quite believing it.

"Me and the mortgage company."

"It doesn't add up, Shelby."

"What doesn't add up?" she asked, exasperation in her voice. The tote bag was slipping off her shoulder, and the hook of the garment bag was torturing her fingers.

"This building, that fancy car you drive, the clothes you wear, that slice of Fort Knox you're wearing around your neck."

There was an implication in the ugly tone of his voice. She dropped the tote and the garment bag on the chair, tossed her portfolio on top of them and crossed her arms over her waist. "If there's something you're trying to say, I wish you'd say it. Is this some sort of accusation?"

"You've been using me. You haven't played straight with me."

"Do you usually get a list of assets from a woman before you get involved?"

"You must have laughed at me, at my gullibility, falling for that line about how much you needed this account, and how desperate you were to keep Caesar as a client."

Unthinking, she reached up and touched his cheek with her fingertips. "I've never laughed at you, Austin. I would never do that."

He swept her hand away, and she felt as though she'd received a punishing physical blow. "Don't waste your time, Shelby. It won't work anymore. Amazing as it must seem, I'm not falling for the struggling young entrepreneur act anymore. I was a little slow catching on, but I'm not stupid."

Shelby didn't know what to do in the face of his anger. She didn't know how to handle him, what to say. She wanted to touch him, feel his arms around her, but he clearly didn't want her touching him. "Austin?" she said sadly.

He turned his head away from her. If he looked at her he'd be lost, drowned in the sorrow in her eyes.

Finally she turned away from him, staring at the wall and hugging herself. She was cold inside, cold and empty.

The silence in the room grew into an ominous, oppressive presence. The sound of their breathing seemed oddly amplified. Shelby inhaled raggedly, trying not to give way to tears. Austin swallowed. The terrible silence went on and on, second after agonizing second.

It was the silence that broke Shelby. She could bear it no longer. Right or wrong, good or bad, she had to end it.

"If we're going to Gainesville, we've got to leave now," she said.

Chapter Seven

She turned, faced him, refusing to wince, not fully understanding what was happening. She had focused on business because if she didn't focus on something she'd have flown apart, or collapsed, or shattered into tiny fragments.

"You said you'd go," she said. "No matter how you feel about me, you're committed to going today."

Austin scowled at her. He opened his mouth, closed it again, grabbed the garment bag and tote from the chair and growled, "Come on. We wouldn't want to be late."

Shelby knelt on the floor and gathered the papers and pens that had skittered in all directions when her portfolio had fallen to the floor. After shoving them haphazardly back into the case she scurried out the door Austin had just exited with the force of a speeding locomotive. He had already hung the garment bag on the clothes hook in his car and was sitting behind the wheel, his fingers drumming an impatient tattoo on the dash. The door on the passenger side was flung open, and Shelby hurried to the seat, mumbling under her breath, "I guess we're taking your car today."

Seconds after she'd put on her seat belt Austin gunned the engine to life and immediately backed out of the driveway and into the street. He sat stiffly, staring straight ahead through the windshield, concentrating on the traffic.

Hoping he wasn't planning to plunge her side of the car into a convenient tree, Shelby sat back and tried to restore order to the hodge-podge of papers in her portfolio.

The traffic was not heavy at that hour on a Saturday, but there still was a noticeable difference when they left the city for the open highway. Austin relaxed visibly, and Shelby felt a glimmer of hope that they might endure the long drive to Gainesville without losing their sanity. She came across the bonus check from Mr. Caesar and slipped the rent check from Laura into the envelope with it. "I've *got* to go to the bank soon," she said, not realizing she was thinking aloud.

"Did you say something?" Austin demanded.

"Nothing," she said. "I wouldn't dream of saying anything."

Austin was sick inside. She'd been an illusion all along, one he'd needed desperately to believe in because he'd met her at such a vulnerable time in his life. Something had been nagging at him about her, but he'd refused to see it. "How far would you have gone, Shelby?"

"I don't know what you mean."

"You got me cheap," he said. "A few kisses. How far would you have gone?"

She glowered at him, unwilling to believe that he was saying such ugly things to her.

"I stopped too soon," he said. "I could have had it all, couldn't I?" He laughed bitterly. "To think I wanted you so badly and was being so noble about not rushing you into bed."

Angry and humiliated by his words, Shelby snapped, "If you weren't driving I'd slap your face for that."

The oppressive silence descended between them again, and the car covered mile after mile of highway. Shelby resisted the urge to roll down the window and scream into the wind.

"Is it Caesar?" Austin's unexpected words cut through the silence like a knife. "Is he the one keeping you?" he persisted ruthlessly. "Is that why it was so important for you to please him?"

She couldn't take any more. She simply *could not* withstand any more abuse. Bursting into tears, she pleaded, "Austin, don't do this. You don't know what you're talking about."

"You've got about sixty miles to explain it to me," he said, purposely not looking at her. If he looked at her he'd be lost to the tears he knew were running down her cheeks, and he'd been suckered by her too many times already.

She rummaged in her portfolio for her purse-size pack of tissue and blotted her eyes, sniffing. "I never lied to you," she said.

He grunted skeptically, and a muscle tensed in his jaw.

"You've put two and two together and come up with three," she said. "Ramon Caesar is not keeping me. No one is."

"You're not hurting, lady. Don't try to tell me you have a money tree in your backyard."

"In a way I do. I told you Caesar's account was important to me, and it is. You just assumed it was important because of the money I'd make from it. It was the success I needed, the feeling of accomplishment."

"Accomplishment doesn't pay for expensive cars and Winter Park duplexes."

"Being a Thurston does."

Austin steered the car to the right sharply and slammed on the brakes. How could he have been so stupid? He turned off the engine, but continued staring out the windshield. "Thurston as in Thurston Enterprises."

"Inc.," she said. "Thurston Enterprises Incorporated."

He still felt angry that Shelby was not the nice, uncomplicated young woman he'd thought she was. The rules had been changed in the middle of a game, but he had leaped to an ugly, unfair conclusion, and he was sorry for that.

Finally he faced her. "I'm not driving now. And I wouldn't blame you for slapping my face."

She shifted in the seat uncomfortably and frowned. "Would that accomplish anything?"

"It would make me feel better."

She stared out the side window. "You don't deserve to feel better."

"You're right. I . . ." He sighed wearily. "I'm sorry for what I said about you and Caesar."

"It was a sorry thing to say." She faced him, and fury flashed in her eyes. "It was an even sorrier thing to *think*." Her bravado faded into a pitiful sadness. "How could you think that of me, Austin? You believed it. Really believed it."

"I was hurt," he said. "And jealous."

"Because you believed it."

"Damn it, Shelby, wanting you is driving me crazy and the thought of another man having you when I couldn't—I couldn't deal with it."

"There was nothing to deal with."

He reached for her and grumbled an obscenity as the seat belt restricted him. He unbuckled it and slid toward her. She was limp as a rag doll as he put his arms around her and hugged her against him. "Forgive me, Shelby."

After a very long time, she said, "It's still fifty-five miles to Gainesville."

When they were on their way again, Austin switched on the radio. Music stabbed at the silence without actually penetrating it. Shelby leaned her forehead against the side window and closed her eyes, trying to sleep, trying to erase the episode from her memory and ignore the pain in her heart.

For twenty minutes, neither of them spoke. Then Austin

said, "You might have told me that you were . . ."

"Wealthy?" Shelby supplied the word he'd stumbled over. "Am I supposed to wear a badge that says, 'One of *the* Thurston Enterprises Thurstons'?"

"It just takes a little getting used to, you know? I thought The Shelby Agency was all you had."

Regarding him through narrowed eyelids, she said, "The Shelby Agency is the only thing I've ever done entirely on my own."

The intensity in her voice scared him a little. The remaining miles to Gainesville were long ones.

They wound up in another broom closet since Shelby couldn't go into the men's room to help Austin with his toga, and he refused to run around the hallways in his tunic.

Affecting normalcy was difficult after the awkward trip. They were aware of the physical closeness the small area imposed on them and were constantly mindful of the fact that they were within touching distance. As Shelby draped the toga over Austin's shoulders, brushed his hair and swirled it around the wreath, she wondered if he felt her fingers trembling, wondered when she had broken her own rule and let Austin get close enough to hurt her. She *was* hurt, and angry and sad—victimized because she had allowed herself to care for Austin and trust him and he hadn't ever really trusted her.

Always before, the sexual tension between them had been exhilarating. The air had crackled with fun because they enjoyed being together. Now the sexual tension made everything awkward, and the fun had drained from it like the air from a beach ball that had been kicked too hard. The easy camaraderie, the coziness, the unstrained frivolity were gone.

Austin's features were stoic, as if chiseled in wood, and he felt like an empty shell. He knew, beyond doubt or reason, that Shelby was the only person who could fill up the new emptiness.

"Finished," Shelby said, stuffing the hairbrush back into the tote bag. There was a finality about the grating sound of the zipper as she closed the bag.

Austin stood up and folded the now empty garment bag Shelby had spread over a crate to protect the toga. She was already at the door, and he reached around her to turn the knob, then hesitated. "Will it ever be the same between us?" he asked.

Shelby sighed. She didn't, couldn't look at him. "I don't know," she answered quietly.

He put his hand on her upper arm, savoring the smoothness of her skin under his. "We can't just let it go."

Gently, firmly, she tugged her arm away.

Austin had little time to think about the hollow ache of losing her once he'd opened the door and stepped into the hallway. The secretaries at the trade show had been slightly uninhibited and in a festive mood, but age had tempered their silliness. Freshmen coeds were a force to be contended with. Their eyes widened, they giggled. Attempts at subtlety were undermined by their sheer inexperience. They were transparent even when they were trying to be subtle, and overpowering when they chose to be obvious.

Added to the craziness was an element Austin had not had to endure at the trade show: freshman boys. The coeds giggled and cooed and sighed. The male students snickered and wisecracked and cast disparaging, superior looks in his direction.

None of the students said, "You can sharpen my pencil anytime, Caesar." At least half a dozen held their new pencils in front of their eyes and admired them as they would an object of art, and said, "Awesome! I'm going to shop at

Caesar's." Shelby noted with grim satisfaction that Mr. Caesar would be pleased.

Lunch was a strained half hour spent in the car under a shade tree behind a hamburger stand trying to pretend there was nothing they had to pretend. On the drive back to campus Shelby wondered how she'd make it through the afternoon.

Angie Collingsworth was in the first group of people to stop at the booth when they returned from lunch. She was a petite girl with blue eyes the size of small lakes, a kitty-cat nose and a proliferation of fluffy, baby-fine blond curls. She appeared always to speak around, through, or in spite of, the giggles continuously spilling forth from some reservoir inside her. Clamping her manicured fingers around Austin's forearm, she said, "You really look like Caesar."

Smiling grimly, Austin delivered the stock line: "May I sharpen a pencil for you, compliments of Caesar's Office World?"

Angie giggled. "Sure." The pencil sharpener whirred, Austin held the pencil in front of her. Taking it, she said, "Are you a student?"

Austin cocked his head to a regal angle and said, "I'm Julius Caesar."

Another wave of giggles. "I meant really." She had entwined her arm around Austin's and was flagrantly batting her long, mascara-coated eyelashes at him. Austin extracted his arm from hers and offered to sharpen a pencil for the next coed in line.

Angie's arm had snaked around his again before the next girl had accepted her pencil. "I did a research paper on Ancient Rome in high school, so I know *all* about you."

"Not everything, I hope," Austin said. Shelby, who'd been watching the entire exchange, noticed that his smile suddenly looked more genuine, less forced.

"You *really* look like Caesar. You're not a history professor, are you?"

For the first time all day, Austin laughed. "No."

"Too bad," Angie said, giggling and batting furiously. "History's my favorite subject."

Something snapped inside Shelby, she didn't know what. But she did know that she'd like nothing better than to deliver a right cross to that mouth with its bowshaped lips covered with three layers of lip gloss. Slapping a pencil into the hand Angie wasn't monopolizing, she said sharply, "Your subjects await, Emperor. You have pencils to sharpen."

Austin focused his full attention on Shelby, his eyes boring into her with incredulity, as though she'd just flung off all her clothes and announced she was going to fly home. Shelby met his gaze unflinchingly, her brown eyes glowing with defiance.

A lazy smile played at his lips. "Yes, ma'am," he said, elongating the words. Withdrawing his arm from Angie's grasp, he turned to a coed with spiked hair who was wearing a punk rock T-shirt, no bra and several heavy leather belts.

Aiming a scowl at Shelby that could have doused the eternal flame, Angie told Austin, "See you later, Dictator," and sauntered away with a pronounced sway of her little derriere. Color crept from Shelby's chest to her neck and higher, stinging her cheeks and burning her scalp.

The braless coed in the garish T-shirt had walked off with her pencil. "College campuses are so stimulating, aren't they?" Austin said.

Snubbing him, Shelby turned to a couple who had just reached the booth, a pretty girl with a heart-shaped face and a tall, lanky boy in a sports jersey. "Would you two like a pencil, compliments of Caesar's Office World?"

"I believe that's my line," Austin said, deftly taking the

pencils from her hands and shoving one in the sharpener. He grinned affably, irritatingly, as the machine noisily gobbled wood. Shelby allowed herself a small, wry smile, and the tension between them slackened appreciably.

The traffic through the booth slowed, picked up, and slowed again. Austin was wandering around the booth restlessly, and Shelby was frowning at a chip in her nail polish when a piercing screech resounded throughout the building. Seemingly from nowhere, a student dashed up to the booth with his arm extended full length above his head.

Shelby recognized the general outline of a knife in his hand as the boy emitted another yell and thrust the weapon into Austin's chest. She did not hear the wail that came from her throat as she lunged toward the kid, thrusting her arms around him. Clinging to him with her left arm, she formed her right hand into a fist and beat at his shoulder blade mindlessly, stopping him her only thought.

Austin's arm snaked around her waist from behind like an iron band, pulling her away. His right hand caught hers, pulled it against her body to still it. "Shelby, it was a joke. A joke."

She twisted her head around, stared at him wide-eyed and uncomprehending. "It was a joke," Austin repeated, holding up the plastic stage knife and demonstrating its retractable blade by pressing on the point.

Shelby resumed breathing and turned a wrathful look at the kid, finally recognizing him as a wise-cracking campus clown who had passed the booth a number of times, always with some snide quip to fling at Austin. "You little . . ." she muttered through clenched teeth, but Austin put a hand on her arm to quiet her.

He tossed the toy knife to the student, now very subdued and obviously relieved to be escaping with minimal bodily injury. "Better luck next time, Brutus."

"What's going on here?" queried a gruff, authoritative voice. All eyes turned to the uniformed security guard. "I had a report there was a disturbance," he said. The kid, already subdued, paled pitifully.

Austin shrugged. "It was nothing, officer. Just a little theatrics."

Still shaken and embarrassed, Shelby started to intervene and demand that the juvenile delinquent be carted off to jail, but the expression in Austin's eyes stopped her, and she saw the folly in making a big deal of the prank.

The furor created by the shouting and fisticuffs died immediately, and they returned to the booth. "Jerk!" Shelby said, following the kid's back with her eyes as he disappeared in the crowd.

Stepping behind her, Austin kneaded her shoulders with his hands and knots of tension melted beneath his touch. "Can't say this job is dull," Austin said.

"I thought he had killed you."

"I'm just glad he didn't try to *pinch* me," Austin said dryly. "He'd have really been in trouble."

He stepped forward to greet three coeds who'd just paused in front of the booth. "May I sharpen pencils for you ladies, compliments of Caesar's Office World?"

Business picked up to a pleasant, manageable pace, closing time drew near and Shelby began to feel that she might survive the terrible day with some remnants of her tattered nervous system still intact. *Just a few more minutes,* she thought, idly surveying the crowd of milling students. Then her expression hardened noticeably. Austin heard the expletive she muttered under her breath and turned to her, cocking his eyebrow questioningly.

"Don't look now, but Goldilocks is on her way back."

Angie's lilac perfume and her giggle reached the booth before she did. She had a friend with her, a quiet, brown-haired girl. Angie clasped Austin's arm urgently and announced, "We've decided to have a toga party."

"That sounds like fun," Austin said noncommittally.

"You're going to be our guest of honor."

"I don't know about that."

"You can't say no!" Angie said. Shelby wondered if her eyelids got sore from the exertion of lifting so much mascara so often. "My sister is a senior and she has an apartment just off campus, and it's all set for tonight. She's calling all her friends to tell them about you. You've just *got* to come."

"Look, Angie, I'm flattered, but—"

"You just *have* to be there. Everybody's going to wear togas, and we're having wine."

"It doesn't sound as if you need me."

"But you're the reason we're having the party. You're Caesar."

"Angie, I've got to leave for Orlando as soon as the show closes. I couldn't possibly stay here for a party."

"You could stay at my sister's apartment tonight. We wouldn't bother you." A froth of giggles spilled from her as she made eye contact with the girl with her. "Not much, anyway."

The pencil sharpener whined, and Austin caught sight of Shelby operating it. The line of students waiting for pencils was backing up. He tugged at his arm, trying to extract it from Angie's grasp tactfully.

"Angie, I can't stay for the party. I didn't come alone. Miss Thurston rode with me."

He did not have to clarify who Miss Thurston was. Angie glared at Shelby as if she were a mass murderer. "She's your boss, isn't she?"

Austin couldn't help smiling at her transparent hostility. "She's the lady who hired me," he said flatly.

Angie harrumphed indignantly.

"Pardon me for eavesdropping," Shelby said, "but I couldn't help overhearing. Austin, if you want to stay in Gainesville, I'm sure I can manage to get back to Orlando on my own. I wouldn't want to spoil your fun."

If a single look could kill, she'd have been struck dead instantly by the wrath in Austin's eyes. "Don't be ridiculous, Miss Thurston," he said, thrusting the words through clenched teeth. "I couldn't leave my boss stranded in a strange city."

"You could come, too," Angie said, almost choking on the words.

Shelby spoke as to a small child. "I'd love to, darling, but I didn't bring a sheet."

Austin shook his head resignedly. "Sorry, Angie."

"It's going to *ruin* our party," she said petulantly.

Sliding his arm across her shoulders, Austin spoke to her in low, confidential tones. "Angie, a pretty girl like you doesn't need me to have fun. Just put on your toga and make up your mind to have a good time with your friends and you will." He gently nudged her toward the aisle. "I've got to work now, Angie. And you've got a party to get ready for."

He took the liberty of putting his hands around Shelby's waist as she sharpened a pencil. When she extracted the pencil from the machine, he took it from her with his right hand, leaving his left hand firmly planted on her waist. "Compliments of Caesar's Office World," he said, presenting the pencil to a waiting coed.

As he took a new pencil from Shelby, he said under his breath, "I should have left you high and dry for not helping me out of that."

"I'd have rented a car."

"A Cadillac?" he asked, baiting her.

"A Rolls!" she snapped.

"Undoubtedly."

The manager of the local Caesar's store arrived to dismantle the booth, and she announced cheerfully, "It's five o'clock."

"Thank God," Shelby muttered.

Chapter Eight

"What was it like for you, growing up?"

Shelby looked across the car and studied Austin's profile in the twilight streaming through the car windows. They had gotten through dinner by sticking to safe, impersonal topics of conversation, and the silence in the car since they'd started on the return drive to Orlando had been a comfortable one. Austin's personal question, though posed gently, was unexpected.

She smiled pleasantly. "If you're expecting a poor little rich girl story, you're going to be disappointed. My childhood was perfectly normal."

"I wasn't expecting anything, Shelby. I'm asking because I don't know and I'm interested. Do you have any brothers or sisters?"

"Three brothers. My parents had two boys, then tried for a daughter, all three years apart. My baby brother came along six years later, quite by surprise."

"Sounds normal enough."

"Thurston Ranch was a wonderful place to grow up. There was always something going on, and plenty of room to grow. My grandfather lives in the main house, and each of his three children, including my father, built on the fringes of the property." She grinned. "Upwind of the cow pastures, of course."

"One would hope so," Austin agreed. "It sounds like your family is close."

"Oh, yes. The Thurstons are thick as thieves and about as numerous. We do our share of fighting, but we're basically a solid clan. In a way it was like belonging to a social club with all the cousins converging at the stables or the pool. Each of us got a pony when we were five and a car when we were sixteen. In between, the traditions were rather vague."

"Did you feel pressured because of who you were?"

She sighed, thinking about the question. "Certain things were expected of us, good grades, for one. We were supposed to go to good colleges so that if we went to work at Thurston Enterprises there would be no question about our qualifications."

"Of course there was never any suggestion of nepotism."

Shelby bristled at the sarcasm in his voice. "Thurstons get a chance at Thurston Enterprises, not a free ride," she snapped.

"I didn't mean—"

"Oh, yes, you did. And no matter how bitter you are over Mason Engineering, you have no right to assume that Thurston Enterprises is run the same way."

"I seem to be making a lot of erroneous assumptions lately."

"No argument."

He reached for her hand, covered it, squeezed it. "I'm going through a bad time, Shelby, and it's been a wretched day. I don't want to argue with you or foul things up any worse than they've already gotten."

Her sigh seemed to reflect his mood. "I feel the same way."

"Then tell me some more about what it's like being a Thurston."

She inhaled then exhaled raggedly. "There's a mystique about being from a well-known family. Sometimes it's like living under a microscope. If you do something well, people know about it, and if you fall flat on your face there are people just waiting around to celebrate the fact that a Thurston can be a failure."

She paused. "I suppose the biggest disadvantage of having a 'name' is that people tend to diminish your accomplishments. No matter what you do, you did it because you were a Thurston with all that money and power behind you."

She shifted in the seat, folding her legs to sit Indian-style. "I can give you a perfect example. In college one girl started a rumor that I'd bought my bustline at a plastic surgeon's."

She laughed wryly. "*That* was a tough one after I'd had to contend with being the most fully developed girl in the class since sixth grade. But it was so typical. I was beautiful because I could afford good cosmetics, my hair was healthy because I could afford good salons and my nail polish didn't chip because it was the best brand. No one stopped to notice that I wore very little makeup, or that I inherited thick, dark hair from my Cuban grandmother, or that I bought my fingernail polish by color and not by brand."

"Your grandmother was Cuban?"

"It was the scandal of the season. My grandfather met and married her on his graduation trip to Cuba and brought her home. My great-grandfather almost threw them both off the ranch, and they fought like cats and dogs, but my grandfather was as stubborn as my great-grandfather, and they were really very close so Pappy finally agreed to accept my grandmother into the family. And of course he fell in love with her too, in a paternal way, and anyone who made a crack to Pappy Thurston about Consuelo Thurston or her heritage got a jawful of Thurston fist or a Thurston boot in the seat of the pants."

"So that's where you got it," Austin said, grinning.

"My dark hair?"

"No. Your aggressive streak."

"I'm assertive, but I'm not particularly aggressive."

"Tell that poor kid you were beating on today. He's bound to be black and blue."

"That was just a dose of cattle ranch justice. I thought I was apprehending a felon."

"Nevertheless, I'm glad I was driving this morning when we were arguing."

"I don't care to discuss anything that happened on this whole miserable day," Shelby said. She leaned her head against the window and closed her eyes, determined to go to sleep. Seconds later she adjusted her shoulders fussily, trying to find a comfortable position.

"I know you're not feeling especially friendly toward me right now, Shelby, but I don't have any communicable diseases, and I'm bound to be softer than that pane of glass."

"Well, if there's one thing a Thurston likes, it's comfort," she said and swiveled in the seat to put her head against his arm, wrestling with the strap of the seat belt until it no longer cut into her. For want of anything else to do with it, she stretched her right arm across her lap.

A contented smile played at Austin's lips as he lifted his arm and draped it over her, giving her cheek access to the cradle of his shoulder. A few minutes later he heard the subtle change in her breathing and felt the difference in her weight against him as she fell asleep.

Austin was reminded of the Christmas puppy he'd kept inside his coat, the special warm joy of holding it next to him knowing it was his. Holding Shelby was far more special than that remembered magic. He wished she were his, or at least that he could be sure there was a chance she would be.

All too soon for him, the trip was over. The stop-and-start city driving woke Shelby, and she sat up and stretched. "I should have put that shoulder on your résumé."

"I usually don't share it with my employers."

It was the last thing either of them said until they reached the duplex.

Shelby opened her own door and started collecting her things from the back seat. "I . . . uh, think I can make it in on my own."

Austin had walked around the car and was standing next to her when she straightened with her arms full. Lifting the tote bag from her shoulder and relieving her of the garment bag, he said, "Don't be ridiculous. How would you get the door unlocked with your hands full?" The look in his eyes checked the protest she was about to make. "You really don't want me inside, do you?"

He was hurt; she could hear the raw misery in his voice. But she was hurt too, dammit. He had hurt her. Now she was confused. "I . . . it wouldn't be a good idea, Austin."

"I'll throw these on the nearest chair and leave," he said. "If you'll go for a walk with me."

"A walk?"

"Sure. You know, you just sort of follow the sidewalk and enjoy the fresh air and talk."

"Talking's the catchy part," she said solemnly.

He put his hand on her elbow as they walked to the door. "We don't have to talk then." He stopped and looked down into her eyes. "I just want to be with you awhile, Shelby." She nodded, and the coil of tension in his chest eased substantially.

The hot day had given way to a pleasant night, and a full moon shimmered brightly in the sky, beautifully flanked by fluffy, translucent clouds. Austin and Shelby didn't touch at first, or talk, but they were very aware of each other's presence as they strolled aimlessly down the sidewalk listening to chirping crickets and an occasional barking dog.

Conflicting emotions pulled at Shelby. She remembered the welcome feel of his hands on her waist while she worked in the booth, the wonderful coziness of his shoulder under her cheek, the warmth in his eyes when he'd smiled at her on better days. But there were other memories, too: the absolute terror she'd felt when she thought he had been stabbed and the searing pain that had cut through her when he'd accused her so unfairly.

They seemed, suddenly, far apart in perspective. She wasn't worried that Austin might be fortune hunting, but her Thurstonism, as she sometimes called it, had become a factor in their relationship. Relationship? That was the most troubling riddle of all. How could a week and a half of camaraderie be considered a relationship? The word sounded so imposing, so serious, not at all like a casual flirtation or pleasant friendship.

The turmoil, the emotional chaos were closing in on her. Austin had said they didn't have to talk, but of course, that was idiotic. They *had* to talk. They weren't going to reach any conclusions or divine any answers, but one of them had to be courageous enough to bring up the subject they were avoiding so they could at least acknowledge that this thing called their relationship existed.

By promising her they wouldn't have to talk, Austin had set the responsibility for introducing the subject squarely on her shoulders. Glancing up at the billowing clouds overhead she said, "Do you think it rained this afternoon?"

"Probably," Austin answered. At least they were talking. He'd begun to think he wouldn't be able to stand the strain of waiting for Shelby to say something. The hell of it was, now he had to wait for her to get around to bringing up the subject they needed to talk about.

Several minutes passed. Crickets continued to chirp; an air-conditioning unit in a nearby yard sputtered to life; their feet made muted scraping sounds on the pavement. Anticipation festered inside them. It gnawed at Shelby until finally she said, "It was happening too fast, Austin."

Austin shortened his stride to match her slower pace. "We can't let it slip away, Shelby. It's too precious."

Shelby stopped, and she and Austin faced each other, their faces pale in the silver moonlight. "I'm not sure there's anything to slip away."

He curled his fingers around her upper arms, willing her to listen to him, believe him. "There's something undeniable between us, Shelby. It's real and strong and special." Looking deeply into her eyes, he added, "And sweet."

Shelby had to steel herself against the effect he was having on her senses. She felt a tingling awareness of his presence, his touch. She forced a harshness to her words. "It wasn't sweet this morning."

"No. This morning . . ." Massaging the back of his head, he heaved a weary, resigned sigh and said, "This morning was a mistake."

"What happened this morning was inevitable," she said softly. "We don't know each other, Austin. How much could we learn about each other in less than two weeks?"

"Everything we need to know."

She shook her head sadly. "No. We've been seeing what we needed to see in each other, dealing with images instead of reality. Reality had to get in the way sooner or later. If it hadn't been this morning, it would have been tomorrow or the next day."

His hands tightened on her arms urgently. "You're not some image I'm responding to. I know you, Shelby. Maybe I didn't know anything about your background, but I know about you, and what you're like."

Jerking her arms away from him, she said, "Is that why you thought I was being kept by one man and seducing another into working for me? You as much as called me a—"

He thrust his arms around her, clasped her to him. "Don't say it, Shelby." He sighed raggedly. "Forgive me. I didn't believe it. I was just surprised and . . . scared."

She pulled away from him. "You were scared because you found out something about me that was incompatible with the image you had of me. If you had really known me, you wouldn't have been so quick to question my integrity. Integrity? Hell! My basic morality."

"You've made your point," he said. "I've admitted that I was wrong and I've apologized. I'd bleed for you if it would do any good."

"That's a little melodramatic, isn't it?"

He grabbed her arms again and thrust his face near hers. "I'm exaggerating to make a point. In case you missed it, it's that I care about you, Shelby Thurston, and I think you care about me. Please don't let one mistake—"

"I can't just push a button and forget being hurt." Not when she'd been hurt before; not after she'd vowed never to let herself get hurt again.

"You care about me, Shelby," he pleaded.

Yes. She cared about him. She cared too much. Her caring had made her vulnerable. "I don't know how I feel," she said miserably, knowing but not wanting to admit it to herself. "I—"

Before she could say another word, his arms were around her, his lips were on hers. The kiss was long, deep, demanding, devastating. She grew weak with the intensity of the sensations, and his strength supported her. She was aware of a hand spanning the small of her back, of his fingers threaded through her hair. His chest was firm against her breasts, his thighs warm and strong where they touched hers, his desire for her evident as his body pressed close to hers.

An answering desire raged through her, frightening in its intensity. Panic gripped Shelby. She couldn't feel this way, couldn't want him like this. He'd already hurt her. She couldn't let him hurt her again, couldn't let him become even more important to her.

Driven by the need not to succumb to him, torn because she wanted him to love her, to make love to her, she wedged her hands between their bodies and shoved at his chest, pushing him away from her. Before he could react to the sudden shove, she spun around and fled, walking briskly in long strides toward the safety of her home. Safety not from Austin, but from the desire he stirred in her, safety from the emotional vulnerability of caring for him, the desire she felt for him.

Austin called her name. She heard the sound of his footsteps behind her and walked faster, almost running. A dog barked angrily from behind a wooden fence as she rounded a corner, startling her, making her hurry even more. Mindlessly, she broke stride and ran. Austin's steps quickened behind her, gaining on her. He caught up with her on her driveway and, clasping her arm, stopped her and turned her toward him. Wet streaks shone on her cheeks.

"Shelby," he said, pleading. He had to know what was wrong, why everything between them was crumbling, eroding away. He grasped both her arms, but she wouldn't look at him. She just kept staring down at her hands. "Tell me, Shelby," he said urgently. "Tell me what's wrong."

Still winded from the exertion, she was breathing heavily. An eternity passed for both of them before she raised her head to face him. "I guess you think that because I'm a spoiled little rich girl, everybody thinks I'm beautiful and men think I'm sexy. I suppose you think I'm very sophisticated and that I've had lots of lovers."

Austin opened his mouth to speak but didn't know what to say. The wrong thing would worsen the situation, and her misery was so obvious, so evident, so gut-wrenchingly pitiable that he couldn't bear hurting her further. He stared down at her tear-stained face, wanting to hold her, to drive away her pain. But when he moved to embrace her, she pulled away, looked up at him with raw misery etched on her face and said, "Well, it's not true. And that only goes to show you how little you know about me."

Spinning away from him, she dashed to the door and disappeared behind it. The click of the lock resounded through the still night air. Austin knocked on the door, quietly at first, then more forcefully. "Shelby," he called, and waited.

"Go away, Austin." Her voice, muted by the barrier between them, sounded expressionless and flat.

"I'm not going away," he said. "I can't leave you like this."

Stony silence answered him. He beat on the door again, loudly this time. "I've got to see you, Shelby. I've got to know you're all right. Shelby!"

The lock clicked, the knob turned, the door opened slowly. Austin stepped inside, his eyes fixed on Shelby's face. "See?" she said. "I'm all right." But she didn't look all right. She looked spent, drained.

"I don't want to leave you, Shelby. Not like this."

"I . . ." She swallowed, then paused, and when she spoke, her voice was a raspy whisper. "I need some time to sort things out."

"We can sort them out together," he said, reaching for her. His hands froze in midair as she flinched.

She turned her back to him and sighed wearily. "I have to sort it out by myself."

"I'm not going to just let go of us," he said. "When . . . ?"

"Don't ask me that. I don't know when I . . . when . . ."

He couldn't bear not touching her. He put his hand on her shoulder in a comforting gesture and released his indrawn breath when she didn't shrink away from him.

Silence encompassed them, a powerful, significant silence. Finally Austin said, "I'll go now."

She nodded mutely without turning around. Austin hesitated, then leaned forward over her shoulder to kiss her lightly on the cheek. "Good night, Shelby."

He was all the way to the door before she spun around and said his name. Hand still on the knob, he turned to face her expectantly. It seemed to him that his heart stopped in anticipation. He wanted for her to open her arms to him and call him back to her, needed to hold her close to him and insulate her from the pain.

But it was not to be. "Good night," she said, and he heard the finality in her soft voice.

Chapter Nine

During his time at home, Austin had discovered that the mailman came every day between one fifteen and one thirty-five. At one forty, he hiked to the bank of mailboxes for his mail, noting that the brief outing would probably be the highlight of his day. Yesterday he'd gotten the first response from the résumés he'd been sending out to companies he'd like to work for. Unfortunately, it was one of those we'd-love-to-hire-you-but-we-don't-have-an-opening letters. Maybe he'd get lucky today, Austin thought. Maybe there wouldn't be any mail at all.

No such luck. He frowned at the stack of bills as he carried them inside and opened them at the built-in desk in the kitchen area. The telephone bill was heftier than usual, thanks to the calls he'd been making to friends in the industry in search of job leads. His Exxon bill had only one charge on it, and he recognized the address of a station he frequented. He slid the statement back into the envelope and tossed it into the "to pay" cubbyhole in his organizer and turned his attention to the American Express. Like the phone bill, it was higher than usual. He'd bought a new suit and dress shoes to have on hand in case he was called for an interview.

Running his forefinger down the list of charges, he stopped at a restaurant listing. It was for the night Shelby had met him for dinner after his interview at the headhunter's office.

The image of Shelby in black, white and red flashed

through his mind, a vivid, poignant memory. Uttering a rude oath, he wadded the statement in his hand and thought of Shelby in jeans and shirt, the weight of her full, firm hips on his thighs as she sat in his lap reading his résumé. As always when he thought of her, he saw her again as he'd last seen her, looking very small and vulnerable, tear stains on her cheeks, shoulders squared bravely as she told him goodnight and meant goodbye.

Muttering another oath, he smoothed the wrinkles from the statement as best he could, shoved it back into the envelope, and jammed the envelope into the cubbyhole with the other bills. He'd picked a hell of a time to get involved in a disastrous romantic relationship. His entire routine and lifestyle were disrupted, his self-confidence was eroding. Calls to the headhunter always netted the same reply: Nothing yet, but something could break any day. In other words, "Don't call us, we'll call you." It was still early to expect any responses from most of the résumés he'd sent out. He'd written out the mortgage check and paid the utility bill, and now he had a fresh stack of bills to remind him the well of money he'd taken for granted had run dry. With his accumulated vacation pay and a respectable savings account he was in no imminent danger of bankruptcy, but he wasn't in the mood for logic. No matter what the circumstances, he was unemployed and he felt unemployed. That was gruesome enough without having to deal with a romantic crisis simultaneously.

He needed Shelby, needed her vivacity, her off-beat enthusiasm for life, her way of subtly stroking his ego. He needed her not because he was lonely and disoriented and feeling a little lost, though he was, but because when he was with her he felt whole.

There was a feeling of rightness about being with her, whether they were talking or kissing or just being content in each other's company. He wanted to take her to bed, yes; he was aware of that need every time he thought of her. But he wanted more. He wanted to go to sleep feeling her body against his and wake up to find she was still there. He wanted to hug her tightly while they exchanged deep, private secrets and to banter with her playfully during casual moments.

Forget her, he told himself. Obviously she isn't having any trouble forgetting you. And she's a Thurston. Can't forget that. Eventually she'd marry a proper millionaire and do volunteer work or marry a pauper who devotes himself to lost causes.

Forget her, Austin. Call up Bob Rankin and arrange to meet the bachelor pack somewhere for happy hour. Tie one on. Flirt with the waitress. Hell, you deserve to let loose a little. If you get blitzed, One-beer-a-night Bob'll make sure you get home okay, and when you recover from the hangover you can put all this self-pity behind you. And Shelby Thurston, too. She'll be history.

And hens have teeth, he thought disgustedly. He didn't want to call Bob and the boys. He didn't want to be with a bunch of buddies indulging in masculine revelry. He wanted to be with Shelby, no matter where she was or what she was doing.

He picked up the phone telling himself he was going to call Bob and dialed Shelby's number instead.

The ring of the phone broke Shelby's concentration on the letter contract she was composing. She stopped her work at the computer and listened to the answering machine monitor as her recorded voice said hello and asked the caller to leave a message at the beep. She'd pick up the phone if the call was important.

"Shelby. I . . ." It was Austin's voice.

She groped frantically for the phone, wanting to catch him before he hung up. The curly wire to the receiver was tangled with the cord to the answering machine, and she had to straighten the knots out without pulling the answering machine off the credenza in order to get the receiver to her ear. "Damn!" she muttered as the wires kept coiling back into a convoluted mass that resembled cooked spaghetti. Finally mastering the pile of wire, she got the phone to her ear and said, "Austin?" Did her voice sound normal? When had the lump formed in her throat?

"Shelby? I didn't think you were home."

"The phone wire was all tangled up."

"I was thinking about you." He wanted her to say she'd been thinking about him, but there was a strained silence at the other end of the line.

The pressure was almost unbearable. Shelby was afraid to say anything for fear of saying too much. If she told him she was thinking of him, she might slip up and let him know that she thought of him constantly. She might blurt out that everything reminded her of him. She might even tell him about taking the spaghetti sauce left over from their dinner out of the freezer one night and bawling like a baby because she missed having him there with her. She asked, "Did you get your check?"

Austin frowned. That was Shelby, all business to her mercenary little core. "I got it Friday."

"Good."

"I guess Mr. Caesar was pleased."

Too pleased, Shelby thought. She toyed with the idea of asking him about Saturday and dismissed it. Things were awkward enough at the moment without resurrecting the specter of Julius Caesar between them.

"I'm going stir crazy around this condo," he said. "I

thought maybe you'd like to go to Sea World Saturday and feed the dolphins."

Damn it! Shelby thought. *Why Saturday?* With seven days in the week, why did he have to single out Saturday? "Oh, Austin, I can't Saturday. I have other . . ." She gave up with a sigh of exasperation. "Oh, what the hell? Mr. Caesar's opening a new store in Cocoa, and he wants a living Caesar there for the grand opening."

Austin felt as if a steel band were tightening around his chest. "Do you have one?"

"I interviewed some models yesterday."

He heard the evasion in her voice and pressed, "Have you hired anyone?"

"Not yet. I'm supposed to get back with the agency tomorrow."

"I'll do it."

"Austin!"

"I don't mind, Shelby. I want to see you, and if that's the only way . . ." His sigh was dismal. "I owe you this one anyway."

"I don't know why you'd think that."

"I don't think it, I just feel like I owe you one. Besides, I'm being selfish. The store'll close early, and I can wine you and dine you afterward."

"In some fancy restaurant? You call that getting out?" she said, her heart soaring. "How about wine coolers and sandwiches on the beach?"

"Whatever you want."

"I . . . we . . . the family has a small house near the beach. We can headquarter there."

"Sounds wonderful," Austin said, thinking how trite and lame the remark sounded. Sunset on the beach, a cozy, private beach house to retire to, some time alone with Shelby.

"Wonderful," was inadequate to describe just how good it promised to be.

On Saturday morning, Shelby fussed with her hair, her makeup, her clothes, going back to the mirror several times to make sure her mascara wasn't clumped, that the tail of her tucked-in blouse wasn't bunched unevenly over her tummy, that her lipstick was straight. She opened her tote, checked its contents and fished in her purse for the keys to the beach house. She wanted the trip to Cocoa, the day, the beach, even the weather to be perfect. Any ambivalence about her feelings for Austin Hastings had dissolved when she'd heard his voice. This sense of anticipation was but a symptom of the extent of her involvement with him, she realized. It was not an involvement she'd consciously planned or thoughtfully choreographed, but one which had been forged by sexual chemistry and kindred interests and all those ethereal intangibles that sprang illogically into play between a man and a woman.

The way she felt as she waited for Austin's arrival was enough to make one believe in the myth of a mischievous Cupid flying around shooting arrows at unsuspecting mortals and inflicting them with the foolishness of infatuation. It was spring fever in the last days of summer, romance in the face of impending disaster, folly in the cold stare of logic.

She and Austin were light years apart in perspective and background. He had shattered her trust by not having faith in her integrity. And by caring so much she was making herself vulnerable to being hurt again. Shelby understood all this completely. But she also knew that he would be ringing her doorbell any moment, and she would open the door to him and be exhilarated by the magic of having his arms around her. His kiss would be gentle and sweet and tumultuous and torrid, and he would say he'd missed her, and she'd slide her arms around his waist and tell him that she'd missed him, too.

Under the influence of Cupid's arrows, she was not wise enough to stop it. She didn't know where they were headed or how long it would last, but she would play the fool because it was better being a fool with a man like Austin than being as abysmally alone as she'd felt when he was away.

When the doorbell finally rang, it all happened as she had known it would. After admiring her with his gray-green eyes, he took her in his arms. The magic was waiting for her there, imbuing her with a sense of both promise and fulfillment.

His kiss was gentle and sweet at first. Then it grew more demanding. Shelby felt as if she could spend the rest of her life in his arms, but too soon it was over and they stood, holding each other tenderly.

Austin's voice was as mellow as sun-warmed honey when he whispered, "I don't want to let go of you." Long seconds passed before Shelby drew her arms from around him to caress his face and stand on tiptoe to kiss him lightly on the lips. When her arms snaked around him again, encircling his neck this time, and she clung to him, hugging him fiercely, he knew everything he needed to know.

They left her duplex and went to his car. Rock music blasted from the radio when Austin turned on the engine. Reaching over to adjust the volume, he caught sight of Shelby's wry smile and, shrugging, grinned sheepishly. "I crank it up when I'm driving alone."

"Doesn't bother me," she said. She'd been smiling at the irony that that particular song should be playing, and that the first thing she heard when she got in the car was the admonition, "You might as well face it, you're addicted to love." She was addicted, all right, not to love, necessarily, but to being with Austin.

The drive to Cocoa seemed shorter than the hour it took. Austin reached across the seat to hold Shelby's hand, and though they alternated between spurts of animated chatter and long lapses in conversation, they were comfortable in each other's company even during the most protracted silences.

Austin turned off on A1A, and Shelby directed him to the Thurston beach house. "Actually, it's not on the beach," she said, "but it's been called the beach house ever since I can remember." It was a boxlike, stucco structure in a long row of similar structures. "Nothing fancy," she said, as they crossed the screened porch, "but you can get cleaned up after a day at the beach, and it sleeps multitudes when we set up cots in the Florida room."

It was, Austin had to admit, not fancy. But it was comfortable and spacious and would have proved adequate permanent housing for an average family of four, as many of the identical boxes near it did. While he changed into his tunic, Shelby scurried around opening windows and doors and turning on fans.

"I'll close up and turn on the air conditioning before we leave so it'll be cool when we get back," she told him as he sat down to have his hair styled. "Sorry it's so stuffy. Obviously none of the Thurston clan has been here recently."

"Have you—has your family had it long?" he asked.

"Yes. My grandfather bought it when the grandchildren—my older brothers in particular—were at that rowdy age. At least one arm of the Thurston tribe would show up almost every weekend, and for the kids, of course, the larger the crowd, the more fun we had. Sleeping on the porch was a special thrill."

Stepping back, she appraised her work and announced that the wreath was in place. The toga routine was by now firmly established and Austin stood up, arm extended, to be draped. Shelby unfolded the bottom length of toga to the arm strap, slid it over Austin's wrist and arm into place. The rest of the draping, right down to the pressing together of the Velcro fasteners, was accomplished in less than a minute, a mere fraction of the time it had taken just weeks before when Shelby had worked from the illustrated instructions.

"Did you remember the Band-Aids on your ankle?" she asked.

He grimaced, shook his head guiltily and said quickly, "I don't need them. The leather's softer now."

Shelby put her hands on her hips and gave him an exasperated scowl. "You need a keeper, Austin Hastings! If you get a big fat blister, the salt water'll sting like hell when we get to the beach." Flicking his chin with her forefinger playfully, she said, "I want you at your best when we go romping through the surf."

Snaking an arm around her waist, and clamping her against him, he said huskily, "The only thing you have to worry about is keeping up with me, woman. You have a way of making a man want to beat his chest."

She poked a finger against his breastbone. "That's fine, as long as you remember it's *your* chest you're supposed to beat, Tarzan."

Leering down at her bosom, he said, "No way I could get our chests mixed up. Yours is broader."

"Chauvinist!" she said, eyes bright with mischief as she patted his behind and spoke as she would to a baby. "Just see if I ward off any wanton pinchers today."

"Keep that up and I'll file a complaint about sexual harassment on the job."

"You're complaining?" she asked haughtily, her head cocked at a jaunty angle, an eyebrow raised provocatively.

His other arm slid around her, and he pulled her to him. "No way, lady." He nibbled at her earlobe. "You can pat my behind anytime you want." His lips were just touching her ear as he whispered, "As long as I can return the favor." He punctuated the statement by cupping both his hands over her buttocks.

Pulling away from him and pushing him a step backward at the same time, she said, "You're an exasperating man, Austin Hastings. Now get that boot off."

"I'll take off anything you ask me to take off," he grumbled, settling into a chair and reaching for the laces of his boots.

"You're incorrigible!" she retorted, thoroughly enjoying herself. She couldn't remember when she'd felt so alive, so attuned to life, so exhilarated. Every nerve ending in her body was alert, tingling with an awareness of Austin as a man and of her own womanhood.

She knelt next to his chair, sat back on her haunches and peeled the backing from the bandage. "There's already a raw spot," she said. "In an hour it would have been a full-fledged blister."

His voice, near shouting, startled her. "How darest thou nag an emperor, slave?"

Laughing, she extended her arms and leaned forward, pressing her head against his ankle. "Oh, mighty Caesar, I beg your forgiveness! See, I kiss your feet to prove my humility." So saying she pressed her lips lightly to the top of his ankle, then slowly slid them to the top of his foot with a tiny nibbling motion. Austin made a sound that was part sigh, part sensual groan.

"Shelby!" A voice exploded from somewhere near the door. Her name was said loudly, sternly, in the irate, censuring tone of a parent who's found his child in a naughty situation. But the speaker Shelby and Austin stared at, mute with shock, was a lithe young man barely knocking at the door of adulthood. Tall, dark, strikingly good looking, he was wearing designer tropical pants, a Ron Jon surfer shirt and thick-soled sandals.

Shelby was the first to recover. "David?"

Austin looked from Shelby to the boy and back. "Shelby?" he asked.

The color that had been noticeably missing from the kid's face returned, and then a prodigious blush crawled from the vee visible above the collar of his shirt, up his neck and over his cheeks. "I wondered who . . ." He paused to swallow the lump of embarrassment in his throat. "I didn't recognize the car."

"It's not what it looks like," Austin said, standing up abruptly.

Grasping the full gist of the situation for the first time, Shelby suddenly burst out laughing. Pressing her fingers to her mouth, she struggled for composure and said, "It's too funny." Hugging herself for support, she surrendered to the rollicking laughter bubbling up inside her for a full minute. Then, finally managing to muster enough control to talk, she brushed her hand against Austin's knee, and he took it, helping her up.

"Austin," she said, wiping a tear from the brim of her eye, "this young man who thinks he's interrupted his prudish sister in a very compromising situation is my baby brother David." She turned to her brother. "David, this is Austin Hastings, who has been gracious enough to help me out with a client."

Austin extended his hand to David, stepping out of the unstrapped *calcei* as he moved. Shelby's brother's gaze took in the toga, the laurel wreath and a bare foot planted next to a booted one. He gaped at Austin incredulously, openly, as though he were a sea serpent who'd slithered up from the beach.

"For Pete's sake, David," Shelby said, "shake hands with him, so he can put his other boot on. We have to be at the mall in twenty minutes."

Briefly, while Austin laced his boot, she explained to David about Caesar's Office World and the living Caesar gimmick. "So as long as we were going to be in Cocoa, we thought we'd spend some time at the beach. What about you? Are you here all by your lonesome?"

"Charlie and Steve and a friend of theirs from college are coming later. I came ahead to open up." Still self-conscious, David glanced down at his hands, at the wall, and back to Shelby. "We were planning on staying until tomorrow night, but if . . ." Staring at his hands again he said, "You know the rule. First come, first dibs. If you want us to clear out before dark . . ."

"Don't be silly," said Shelby, sensing Austin's eyes on her face, knowing he was watching the flush spreading over her cheeks. "We're just going to change here before we head home tonight. We weren't planning . . ." She looked at Austin. Or were they?

Austin touched her elbow reassuringly, a signal that they were a team, and he was on her side. He raised his arm and slung it across her shoulders. "Shelby tried to talk me into staying for immoral purposes, but I insisted on defending my honor."

"I cried all the way down here over the rejection," Shelby said dryly, extending the joke. The light touch of humor was exactly right; it sounded casual enough. Friendly, not intimate.

David, visibly relieved, smiled. "I guess we'll see you guys later, then. Steve's stopping for groceries, so there'll be something on hand if you get hungry."

Shelby smiled. "Thanks for the offer, but we're going to

pick something up. And tell Steve hands off the bottle of wine in the fridge."

Laughing, David answered, "Steve hasn't touched wine since Roxanne's wedding."

"Ooo," Shelby said, wincing. "I guess he *would* have a hangover after that."

"Applied aversion therapy," David agreed.

"Serves him right for getting so blitzed," Shelby said and, turning, looped her elbow around Austin's arm. "It's off to the chariot races for us, Caesar."

"The woman is a slave driver," Austin told David.

"Don't get her mad. She has a mean right cross," David advised sagely.

"We certainly gave your baby brother a turn,"Austin said, as he drove toward the mall.

Shelby broke into fresh gales of laughter. "Did you see his face? He was so . . . morally outraged."

"Do you blame him?" Austin said. "Walking in and finding his sister kissing the foot of some weirdo in a toga."

"It must have to do with the male hormones," Shelby said glibly.

"What?"

"The tendency to take everything at face value and jump to all the wrong conclusions."

The rest of the drive was very quiet.

Chapter Ten

The grand opening went well. Mr. Caesar himself was there with a photographer in tow, and he was impressed by Austin's dignified portrayal of the Roman dictator. The crowd, composed mostly of adults, was friendly but subdued, and there were no episodes of pinching or unexpected theatrical stunts. Few women made lewd or suggestive remarks, although many were obviously attracted by Austin's friendly smile.

Mr. Caesar took Shelby aside before leaving and told her again how pleased he was with her idea. Glancing toward Austin, who was smiling down at an enchanted customer, he grinned affably and said, "Now I understand why my sales figures went up after the clerical workers' show."

Shelby nodded her head knowingly. *Sex sells,* she thought. *A truth as constant as death and taxes.*

"By the way, Shelby," Mr. Caesar continued, "I'm sure you saw the photographer at work today. I want to frame some pictures of the grand opening."

"Yes, sir."

"I'll have the proofs Tuesday. If you'd like to stop in for Austin's check, you can take a look at them then."

"I'll plan to do that," she said, and returned Mr. Caesar's paternal goodbye hug. As she walked back to the table where Austin was stationed, she noted with satisfaction that he was watching her, and that the sparkle in his eyes was warm and welcoming and directed exclusively at her. There was a sparkle in her own eyes as they roved over his broad shoulders, bronzed face and hard muscles. Unlike all the women who'd gone through the Caesar's booth and only fantasized about having that lean body next to theirs, she actually would leave with him when the day was over. The thought of it thrilled her.

Looking squarely into his admiring gaze, she smiled fetchingly.

The inevitable afternoon thunderheads darkened the sky as they left the mall, and fat drops of rain splattered the windshield before they reached the exit to the parking lot. "Looks like our picnic on the beach is going to be delayed a bit," Austin said.

"Nonsense!" Shelby said. "By the time we've stopped for the sandwiches and gone back to the house to change it will have passed over."

"Is that a fact?" Austin said, just as a rumble of thunder loud enough to rattle teeth crashed through the atmosphere.

"We may even get a rainbow," Shelby said confidently, certain that not even nature could ruin their time together when she felt the way she was feeling.

The rain had not abated by the time they reached the hole-in-the-wall deli Shelby assured him made the best sandwiches in the world, and it was still pouring when she made the mad dash from the shop back to the car with the sandwiches. "Told you you should wait until the rain let up," Austin said teasingly as she pushed a strand of damp hair from her forehead.

She brushed drops of rainwater from the clear plastic bag that contained the two sandwiches. "Our dinner didn't get wet."

The rain gradually dwindled to a soft drizzle and finally to a few isolated drops, so that they didn't even have to run from the car to the beach house. A blast of rock music and the din of masculine banter greeted them as they opened the door. David and his friends were sprawled on the living room furniture, and the coffee table was littered with soda cans and pretzel bags. They all looked up when the door opened, and a dead lull fell over the conversation as the young men gawked at Austin's costume. Austin bore the scrutiny with dignity, his eyes leveled at them unflinchingly.

"Julius Caesar, I presume?" one of the boys said, relieving the strained silence.

"Only for as long as it takes me to get out of this sheet," Austin said.

"Hard day at the chariot races," Shelby quipped. They fumbled through introductions. Then Shelby put her hand on Austin's elbow and said, "Come on. I'll help you out of that costume."

Her cousin, Steve, cocked an eyebrow at her. "Don't get too helpful, Shelby. Keep a lock on your libido. We'd hate to have to rescue this one, too."

She frowned at him. "Funny, Steve."

Undaunted, Steve continued, "Should have heard that fellow holler. She scared that poor boy so bad we had to lock Shelby in the bathroom after we pried her off him so he wouldn't see her and get hysterical again."

"Was that the mailman or the door-to-door salesman?" Charlie asked.

"The salesman," Steve answered. "Don't you remember? She cornered the mailman in the hay barn out at the ranch."

"Oh, yeah," Charlie said. "That was when she was fifteen, wasn't it?"

"Don't forget the bullfighter and the French chef," Shelby said sarcastically.

"They don't count," Steve said. "The bullfighter didn't

holler for help, and the French chef was able to keep you at bay with a cleaver."

"Ignore them, Austin," Shelby said, taking his hand and leading him toward the bedroom where he'd left his clothes.

"Just holler if you need help," Charlie called after them.

"Don't worry about me; I know karate," Austin called back, and the remark drew a volley of ribald laughter.

"You caught on to Thurston humor in a hurry," Shelby said when they were secreted away.

Austin's arms snaked around her waist. "Why don't you give me a little sample of what reduced the salesman to a quivering pulp?"

"Are you sure your karate's good enough?"

"I'll take my chances."

"Well, there was a little of this," she said softly, slipping her hand inside the folds of the toga. "And a lot of this." Eyes alight with mischief, she worked the tips of her fingers over his ribs fiercely, tickling him.

Bursting into laughter, he grabbed at her wrist. But by the time he had pulled her hand away, she'd worked her other hand inside the toga and was at work on the other set of ribs. "Shelby!" he said exasperatedly. "Shelby, stop it. I swear I'll yell for help!"

"And admit you don't know karate?"

"That did it," he said, finally managing to trap both her wrists in his hands. "You want karate, I'll show you karate."

He stalked to the bed, pulling her along with him, and sat down on the edge of it. Tugging on her wrists, he pulled her across his lap and swatted her behind. She gasped and rolled over in his lap, reaching back to rub her injured pride. "That wasn't karate!" she accused.

He gathered her into his arms and rocked her. "There's karate," he said, kissing her temple, "and there's karate." His lips found hers, covered them, captured them. Shelby forgot everything outside the circle of his arms, the feel of his lean body next to hers, the warm sense of knowing that he cared for her.

After he'd kissed her, she snuggled against him and sighed. "I don't remember that from any of the Bruce Lee movies."

"It's my own version," he said.

"Does it take lots of practice?" Her dark eyes glistened with affection as they peered into his. Austin thought she could probably see all the way to his heart, his soul. If so, then she knew already what he had not told her, had not admitted even to himself. She could see it, was seeing it. The knowledge glowed in her eyes. She was basking in it.

"It doesn't take any practice at all," he said. "It just takes the right inspiration."

"I . . . uh, am supposed to be disrobing you."

"You have my unqualified permission to disrobe me anytime, anyplace."

"It would probably be a good idea if we weren't in here alone too long."

"I know," he agreed, but he hugged her more tightly against him instead of letting her go. "I wish . . ."

"You wish what?" she prompted after a long pause.

He kissed her briefly on the lips. "Right now I wish you were the only Thurston at home."

Shelby gave him a small hug and reluctantly climbed out of his lap. He stood, and she silently unwrapped the toga, folding it in her arms. She put it on a hanger in the garment bag and picked up her beach tote. "I'll meet you in the living room."

She put on her suit, and then, over it, a pair of cotton beach baggies gathered at the waist and rolled up to her knees and an oversized shirt of white cotton lace, which she left unbuttoned and untucked.

Austin, wearing a T-shirt and surfer-style swim trunks, had joined the circle of young men. Shelby couldn't help noticing that he stood out, a man—mature and confident—among boys still struggling to prove to themselves and the world that they had the potential for manhood. The conversation had drifted to the subject of college football, and Charlie was discussing which teams would be included in the pre-season top ten polls. David was the first to see her enter, and he smiled at her meekly. Austin saw her, excused himself from the circle, walked across the room to meet her. "Ready?" he asked.

"You bet. Let's get the wine and the inner tubes and hit the surf."

"You two going to the beach in the rain?" Charlie asked.

"It's not raining anymore," David said defensively.

There was a hint of masculine camaraderie in Austin's grin. "The lady is expecting a rainbow."

"That's no lady, that's just cousin Shelby," Steve called into the kitchen after them.

"She's not my cousin," Austin retorted.

"No kissing then," Charlie called, and a heady round of laughter followed.

"Obnoxiousness is a Thurston family trait," Shelby said under her breath. She'd taken the wine from the refrigerator and given it to Austin. "Open this. We'll have to put it in a thermos. No glass bottles are allowed on the beach."

Minutes later they were off, carrying inner tubes, mats, a picnic basket and towels. The surf was still misty from the recent rain, and the beach was almost deserted. The vendor who rented umbrellas and boards from a wooden trailer had closed shop, leaving the padlocked trailer behind.

The storm clouds had cleared, giving way to blue skies, but already there was a hint of dusk on the horizon. The effect was one of a watercolor wash rather than sharp photography. It suited Shelby and Austin's mood perfectly. They spread the mats side by side and sat down. "Ready for a dip?" Austin asked, pulling his shirt over his head.

Shelby didn't answer, and he looked at her, then followed her fixed gaze to the sky. "You got your rainbow," he said softly, moving behind her and putting his hands on her shoulders.

She leaned against him, tilting her head back to rest it on his shoulder. "It's not just mine," she said.

"You ordered it."

"For us."

It was a wide, full-spectrum rainbow. They watched it until it began to fade. "I don't want to see it disappear," Shelby said. "It would be like losing something."

He squeezed her shoulders tenderly. "How about that swim now?"

She turned and nodded. He stood up, then took her hand to help her up. Sliding her lace shirt off, Shelby folded it and laid it on the mat. Knowing he was watching her and feeling the warmth of his gaze, she pushed the waistband of her beach pants down over her hips, and, bending forward, stepped out of them. She had worn the pants expressly for the effect taking them off would have on him, and she was not disappointed. She half smiled at him, making him aware she knew what was on his mind as his eyes roamed over the high cut of the suit above her thighs and the low vee between her full breasts. Under his gaze she felt beautiful, desirable.

His voice was husky, seductive, its tone suggestive. "Do you know how good you look?"

She smiled enigmatically. "Of course I do. When a woman

is one size on top and a different size on the bottom, she doesn't shop for a swimsuit, she goes on a quest. When I go to all the trouble to find a suit, I don't settle for one that doesn't look good."

You're a vixen today, he thought, enjoying the game of seduction, sensing that she was enjoying it too, and knowing that if the seduction didn't lead to fulfillment soon he'd die from wanting her. The sleek black suit she wore was more provocative than nudity, revealing enough beauty to titillate, hiding enough to let fantasy and imagination run wild. But it was Shelby herself who was driving him mad with her half smiles, with the frank messages flashing in her eyes, and with her advance-and-retreat teasing. Tickling him in the bedroom with her relatives so close, and daring him to do something about it!

Now she had picked up one of the inner tubes and was halfway to the beach, all sleek perfection from head to toe. She turned and waved for him to follow. "Grab an inner tube and come on," she called.

"I'm coming!" he answered, reaching for the float. *I'm coming after you, Shelby Thurston. Full speed ahead. And I intend to have you. You're playing a game I intend to win.*

Hanging in the inner tubes, they bobbed in the surf, letting the gentle waves rock them and the larger waves slap over them. Far up coast, beyond the launch pad at Cape Canaveral, a vividly colored cruise ship set out to sea, eventually passing them in the distance. Twenty yards away, a flock of pelicans floated on the surface of the clear blue water, took flight and then dove into the salt water after fish. Austin and Shelby speculated on where the cruise ship was going, watched the drama of the pelicans' hunting and splashed water at each other as they giggled like children.

Casting the inner tubes aside, they body surfed and cavorted in the water, splashing mirthfully, swimming against the current, racing through the shallow water as the waves nipped at their ankles. A crab skittered past Shelby's foot, surprising her; she squealed and leaped into Austin's arms. Their bodies touched in the water, thigh against thigh, her breasts pressing against his bare chest through the slick fabric of her swimsuit. He pulled her close to him and kissed her. They were lost in passion until a salty wave of sea water swept over them, knocking them off balance. They recovered, sputtering, clawing at the water, laughing at their foolishness in forgetting where they were.

"Race you in," Shelby challenged, but they raced the wind instead, together, hand-in-hand, not caring who won, caring about nothing except being together.

Shelby toweled off, blotting her skin, rubbing her hair in the folds of the towel. She glanced up to find Austin's eyes on her, admiring, appreciating. "How 'bout a sandwich?" she said. "I'm as hungry as you look."

"I'm not thinking about sandwiches."

"I know."

They drank wine out of plastic glasses and devoured their sandwiches as if they were a feast. Everything was colored by the mauve and pink glow of the slowly setting sun. The pounding surf played a symphony, and gulls glided gracefully against the horizon. They were alone except for an occasional tourist, guests at seaside hotels out for their evening constitutionals.

If he could not be alone with her at the beach house, then being with her here in the glow of the sunset was the next best thing, Austin mused. There were questions he needed to ask her, riddles about her to be solved. Today she was warm and wonderful, but on that awful night two weeks ago she had been a quivering mass of raw vulnerability. He had to know why, how she could be stripped of her confidence so thoroughly. There was something inside her, some unresolved pain he'd triggered, and as long as it was there, unresolved, it could rear its head between them again. He didn't mind taking the rap for his own stupidity in hurting her, but he wasn't going to be a convenient fall guy when old emotional wounds ached.

Methodically he ground the scraps from their sandwiches into a neat pile of crumbs. "What are you doing?" Shelby asked.

"Getting ready to feed the gulls." She laughed, a full, voluptuous sound that aroused him. "What's so funny?"

"You," she said. "Only tourists feed the gulls."

He laughed, drew in a deep breath and laughed even harder.

"What's so funny?" she asked.

"You are," he said. "How can you maintain a seed kitchen for half the jays in the state of Florida and begrudge a sea gull a few scraps?"

"I don't stand under the jays when I'm feeding them."

Balancing the pile of scraps on the white butcher paper in his hand, he stood up. "Come on," he said, "live dangerously. If there's a casualty, we have a whole ocean to wash off in."

Austin threw some of the scraps into the air and the gulls came, swooping gracefully to catch them. Shelby finally took some of the crumbs and tentatively tossed them to the birds.

"Aren't you afraid someone will see you?" Austin teased.

"They'll think I'm a tourist," she said, grinning sheepishly.

There were no casualties, and they did not go back into the water, choosing instead to walk along the water's edge, letting the incoming tide tickle their feet. The sun and the tourists had disappeared, a crescent moon had risen, a cool breeze wafted across the water's surface. Shelby shivered. Austin rubbed her arms with his hands. "Cold?"

"I think I could use my shirt," she said, and he got it for her, letting his hands linger on her shoulders after he'd helped her put it on. He kissed her cheek, and she leaned back against him, enjoying the warmth of his body. He pressed his cheek to hers, his day's growth of beard rough against her soft skin, and he reached around to cross his arms in front of her above the lush cushion of her breasts.

Night sounds engulfed them: the pounding of the surf, the distant cawing of birds. Shelby sighed and relaxed even closer against him.

"Shelby?" The apprehension was audible in his voice. She tensed slightly, not wanting anything to intrude on the perfection of the moment.

"Hmm?" she sighed wistfully, a lump forming in her throat.

"This morning," he began, and paused. "When David found us." He felt her nod her understanding. "You said . . . you called yourself his 'prudish' sister. What made you say that?"

Shelby tensed. She didn't want to think about the unguarded comment, didn't want to try to explain it. But he had posed the question and was waiting for an answer, and she sensed that if she didn't try to answer it, something between them would be destroyed. "It was just . . . I've never been much of a swinger, and you met some of the Thurstons. I guess they always made me feel a little prudish."

"Weren't there any other girls in the family?"

"Just Theresa. She was a year older than me. And she was more—" she sighed "—normal, I guess."

He hugged her, comforting her, while he asked a question

that would prod her further. "Define normal for me, Shelby." He felt her shrug, as though trying to shake loose from something that disturbed her.

"She dated all the time and brought guys out to the ranch."

"You dated, too, didn't you? Guys must have been standing in line to date you."

"Yes, but . . ." Her voice trailed off. "Theresa just handled adolescence better than I did. But she didn't have as much to cope with as I did."

"You mean being a Thurston?"

"That was just part of it. It was much more." She twisted in his arms so she could see him. "I think I'd like to sit down."

They settled on the mats, Austin stretched out on his side propping his weight on one elbow. Shelby sat near him, hugging her knees while she watched the moonlight glinting on the waves. "Tell me, Shelby," he said.

Shelby knew he wanted the truth. How could she begin to tell him about the insecurities that had haunted her adolescence? Could she even attempt to explain? Would he understand? Could any man understand? Her gaze fixed on the flight of a lonely gull silhouetted in the pale moonlight.

She was far away from him. Too far. He wanted to draw her back, wanted proof that she trusted him enough to share part of herself with him. "Shelby," he prompted.

"I was an early bloomer," she said. It wasn't what he'd been expecting. He waited patiently for her to continue, watching her profile in the light cast by the slender crescent of a new moon. "I didn't just bloom," she continued, turning to him with a sad smile. "I grew up overnight. Theresa was thirteen, worried that she'd never be able to get out of a training bra, and I was twelve and I'd bypassed training bras a year before." Her eyes sought his. "Are you sure you want to hear this?"

Leaning forward, he kissed her briefly on the lips. "I'm fascinated."

"Theresa worried about her hips being too full, but she had a darling figure. And there I was feeling like Bessie the Cow in front with *nothing* in back." She paused thoughtfully. "It wasn't just Theresa. It was all the other girls, too. At first I was a freak, because no one else had any breasts at all, and then everyone was jealous because I had so much more than they did."

She rested her chin on top of her knees for a moment, thinking, trying to find the best way to express what she was trying to tell him. "It was difficult with boys. They were trying to touch me when I was eleven. I'd slap their hands, and they would laugh, and I'd feel even more like a freak."

The remembered pain was very real in her voice. He wanted to hold her but sensed she didn't want comfort just yet. "I guess as time went on I developed enough resentment to sully the fun. The girls would whisper about sex and speculate what it would be like and I would listen with a morbid curiosity, wondering why they couldn't see that guys didn't care about girls, only about breasts. And they were envious, because the guys all talked about my chest and strangers would whistle at me and yell stuff at me and they all thought it would be super to be so sexy. And I was rich to boot. They didn't think it was fair."

Tears glistened in her eyes. "I couldn't tell them that I hated it all, the catcalls, and the jokes and the cracks. And I hated guys pawing me, trying to get into my blouse, trying to touch me in the crowded halls in between classes. I felt like I was two lumps, and nothing else that I was mattered to anyone but me."

He stroked her cheek with his fingertips. "Couldn't you tell anyone how you felt? Your mother? A friend?"

"And have them tell me how grateful I should be that I was well endowed and how awful it was to complain when I had so much to be thankful for?"

Sitting up, he cradled her face in his hands and then leaned forward to kiss her gently on the lips. She slid her arms around his neck as he embraced her, and they stayed that way for a long time, just holding each other.

"I'm not sure I should be telling you this," she said.

"It's time someone listened without judging you. I'm glad I can be the one." He continued holding her, stroking her back, smelling the salt water in her damp hair. He hated to risk destroying their closeness, but there were still things they had to discuss. "The week before last," he said, "when we had that terrible argument, you said that I probably thought you'd had lots of lovers—"

"I shouldn't have said that. I was just . . . I could tell you wanted to make love and I . . ."

"Tell me," he said, after what seemed an interminable, unbearable pause. "What, Shelby? Why did my kissing you—wanting you—upset you so much?"

"Because I wanted you, too," she said, and he could see the shimmer of tears in her eyes. "I didn't want you to stop kissing me, I didn't want to send you away. But I couldn't let you stay. I was hurt; *you* had hurt me."

"I was an ass."

Her silence was a form of mute agreement, but neither of them wanted to rehash the issue. A very long time passed before Austin spoke again. "You said that I probably assumed you'd had lots of lovers, and that I was wrong. Did you mean that . . ."

A tinkle of soft laughter caught him unprepared. "That I'm a virgin?" she said. "No." She left him again, retreated to that private world of thought. He wondered if she was actually seeing the ocean as she stared off at the horizon. Finally she returned, tilting her head so that her cheek rested on her knees where her chin had been propped. "But there haven't been . . ." She swallowed uncomfortably. "There was a man, in college."

Austin felt knots forming inside him. "Was it a bad experience for you?"

"The lovemaking?" she said, a note of wistfulness in her voice. "It was . . . sweet. He was gentle and patient, and it seemed almost lyrical."

Scowling, Austin said, "I'm not sure I want to hear any more of this."

Her hand caressed his arm. "I'm sorry. But you asked, and it's important, I think. I mean, it's important that you understand that the lovemaking was special so that the rest of it makes sense."

"Go on," he said grimly.

"By the time I got to college I'd gotten past all the nonsense about my bosom, and I had fortune hunters to worry about, so the grabbers didn't seem to be important anymore. I dated. I'd dated in high school, for that matter, but there was never anyone special. There were plenty of guys making grabs, but none that I wanted to be grabbed by."

She paused. "By the end of my sophomore year I was beginning to think . . . all the girls in the dorm talked about their affairs and discussed the pill, and talked about this guy's tush or that guy's shoulders, and I just listened. But I was beginning to feel like a freak again, because I didn't have anything to talk about. No one suspected . . . except the guys I went out with, maybe, and they weren't about to tell anyone they'd struck out. I knew enough about guys from being around my brothers and my cousins to know that." She paused to catch her breath. "And then I met Ken."

"And he was different," Austin said dryly.

"He was a graduate student," she said, ignoring the sarcasm in his voice. Austin had opened this can of worms; let him deal with the squirmy truth. "He was working on his Ph.D. and teaching freshman math. Anyway, he *was* different. We started out as friends, and then started dating, and he wasn't all over me the minute we were alone. By the time he got around to . . . well, I was ready. And I was relieved to know I could feel the way he was making me feel. I wasn't a freak, or frigid, or any of those terrible things I'd imagined. I just hadn't met the right person yet."

Dear God, let him be alive, Austin thought. *If he died tragically no one will ever fill his shoes.*

"We became lovers on Valentine's Day. It was very romantic, and, as I said, he was very gentle and patient. I was thrilled. We were in love, and I imagined spending the rest of my life with him, blissfully happy."

Please, God, let him have turned out to be a fortune hunter.

"He stayed in Florida over the spring break. He really didn't have any reason to go anywhere else, and he had papers to grade and grades to average and he wanted to work on his dissertation."

Austin sensed the change in her as the gravity of remembered heartbreak settled in her heart.

"He was supposed to come to the ranch for Easter. There's always a big egg hunt and picnic."

Please don't let him have been killed in traffic on the way.

Her sigh was heavy, woeful. "He called and canceled. He said he was getting a lot of work done on his dissertation and didn't want to leave it when it was going so well.

"Naturally I felt sorry for him, working so hard."

"Naturally." *Thank you, God.*

"So I packed up leftovers from the picnic and drove up to

give them to him. I was just going to stay a few hours, give him the food and—" Embarrassed, she stopped.

"I get the gist," Austin said dryly.

The flatness of her voice as she continued was just a coverup for the tightness in her throat. He could tell the memory still hurt her. "He answered the door with nothing but his jeans on, and his hair was all disheveled. I thought he'd fallen asleep while he was working, but he acted so strange, and the look on his face was like sheer panic."

"He wasn't alone."

She shook her head slowly. "He'd carried his books down to the beach to work, just for a break, and run into . . . they'd been engaged when they were both undergraduates, but their parents had given them a hard time about it, and it hadn't worked out. He'd even told me about her. How ironic was that? Anyway, they'd got to talking about old times and decided to catch up with each other over dinner, and what they caught up with was the fact that they never should have split up."

A tear spilled over her cheek. "It was awful for everybody. Andrea—that was her name—was embarrassed and I was devastated, and Ken . . . Ken was sad. He felt so guilty. Andrea disappeared into the bedroom so we could talk, and I cried and called him a lot of names, and Ken cried and told me how very sorry he was. He really was sorry, I know that now. He'd never stopped loving Andrea. Their parents had managed to break them up, but now they were older and stronger and they had decided to get married and tell their parents after the fact."

Shelby's eyes fixed on Austin's face. "He cried and told me how sorry he was, and I told him to go to hell and walked out." She sighed and pressed her forehead against her knees, her eyes squeezed shut against the memory. "I'm not very proud of that now, but it was the only way I could handle the pain at the time. I had given him everything. My love . . . my virginity."

Finally, she surrendered to the tears. "I gave him everything, and he threw it all away. He threw *me* away."

Austin collected her in his arms and rocked her, feeling the moisture of her tears on his chest. "I thought I was going to die," she said. "I didn't think I would survive it."

Rocking her, clinging to her fiercely, he said, "But you did. And now you're here. God, Shelby, I'm glad you're here with me."

"But you hurt me, too," she said. "Just by thinking those awful things. And I couldn't . . . not then." She pulled away from him and wiped her eyes. "I lost more than one kind of innocence in that relationship. Trust doesn't come easily to me anymore. Neither does commitment. That includes sexual commitment."

"You can trust me," he whispered. "I would never throw you away."

Sliding her arms around his neck, she hugged him tightly. "You couldn't possibly mean that as much as I want to believe it at this moment."

Chapter Eleven

The magic of their new intimacy was slow to dissolve as they sat on the beach, communicating only through the touch of their bodies as they embraced, but eventually the breeze died down and the mosquitoes began pestering them. Finally they packed up the mats and inner tubes and trekked to the beach house.

There was a shower in the backyard, an inelegant little stall with wood slat walls and a concrete floor, and they stopped to rinse the sand off their feet before going inside.

"That's cold!" Austin said, following Shelby's lead in sticking one foot and then the other under the water spray.

"For hot water you have to wait until you're inside at the real shower," Shelby said.

"You could have warned me," he said.

"Maybe I thought you could use a cold shower," Shelby retorted.

"Maybe we both could!" he said and, grabbing her by the arms, twirled her fully under the stream of cold water.

"Austin! My shirt! That's cold!" His hands went from her upper arms to snake around her, and his lips found hers. Shelby quickly forgot about the cold water as he kissed her.

"I always thought the cold shower theory was a myth," he said, his mouth close to her ear. "Now I know for sure."

Shelby knew, too, because his arousal was obvious in the frank intimacy of their close embrace. But he was not the only one undaunted by the cold shower. "If you're finished experimenting," she whispered, "why don't you turn off that stupid water and just go with the flow."

He kissed her again, thoroughly, properly, and she surrendered herself to the wondrous sensations his kiss evoked. Anticipation grew into a living, active thing inside her, amplifying every exquisite sensation. His kiss titillated; it held the promise of fulfillment. Emotionally she was closer to him than she had ever been to a man, and there was a rightness about that closeness that suited her, soothed her, reassured her.

She was caught up in the maelstrom of emotion and sensation he stirred in her when her name rang through the night, seemingly from a disembodied voice in the darkness. Austin raised his head, she drew hers back, both turned toward the source of the summons.

"Is that you, Shelby?" The voice, this time, was not disembodied at all but connected to her brother David. Shelby took a deep breath and the few steps required to allow her to peep around the wooden wall of the stall.

Even in the mixture of pale moonlight and the pallid glow of a distant street lamp, David could read the irritation in his sister's dark eyes. "I heard the water running, and when no one came in, I decided to see who . . . to make sure it was you guys," he explained defensively.

"We were just rinsing the sand off our feet," Shelby said. It sounded lame, even to her, and she made no effort to explain the fact that her hair and shirt were wet.

There was a strained silence before David asked, "How was the surf?"

"Calm," Shelby replied.

Austin stepped out of the stall and casually draped his arm across Shelby's shoulders. "The lady got her rainbow."

David smiled. "Good."

"Is the whole crew here?" Shelby said, unconsciously moving closer to Austin.

"Just Steve and I. Charlie and his friend are checking out the local night spots."

Shelby slapped at a mosquito. "Why are we standing around out here?"

David shrugged. "Beats me."

Shelby looked at Austin. "There are two bathrooms, but the plumbing does weird things when both showers are running at once. Why don't you go first? It takes me a while."

"Shelby's a marathon showerer," David interjected. "It's a family joke."

"My brothers never could understand that it takes time to shampoo and condition properly."

They had reached the screened porch and David opened the door. Austin paused and looked at Shelby. "Last chance to go first to the showers."

"Go on," she said, laughing softly, giving him a nudge. "That way I won't feel compelled to hurry when it's my turn."

David stopped Shelby as she was about to follow Austin into the house. "Can I talk to you a minute?"

"Sure," Shelby said.

David shifted his weight from one foot to the other timidly. "I just wanted to say . . ." He took a breath. "I'm sorry, Shelby. I just keep . . . interrupting you, and I don't mean to."

Regarding him closely, feeling his discomfort, Shelby sighed. "You didn't interrupt anything, David." *Nothing except, perhaps, the rest of my life.*

He frowned. "Don't treat me like a kid, Shelby. I could tell . . ." He leveled an incisive look at her. "He's different, isn't he? Special?"

She hesitated, knowing she couldn't deny what he'd perceived, but unsure how much to admit. "He's . . . we haven't known each other very long, but . . ."

"He's special." David finished for her, cocking an eyebrow.

"Yes," she said. "But that's not for broadcast on the Thurston grapevine. It's too early, and these things have a way of—" her voice faded "—fizzling out."

"This one won't."

"It won't?" she asked, looking at him skeptically. "Is that a psychic revelation, or did you dig out a deck of Aunt Patty's tarot cards while Austin and I were at the beach?"

"I can just tell," he said defensively. "I may be younger than you, but I'm not a kid anymore. And I'm not blind."

Shelby didn't say anything. David shifted his weight again. "I hope it works for you, Shelby. He seems like a nice guy. And you look happy with him."

Shelby laughed and gave him a hug. How long had it been since everything had seemed so simple? "You're right, David. You're not a kid anymore. But I wish you could stay eighteen forever."

The lateness of the hour, the romp in the surf and the intensity of the day caught up with Shelby in the dark comfort of Austin's car. It felt good to be clean and fresh after being sandy and salty, and it felt good to be isolated from the rest of the world with Austin in his car. Cuddling against his arm, she said, "I seem to recall something about your being comfortable."

He laughed softly and draped his arm over her shoulders, affording her access to his shoulder.

"This really isn't fair to you, making you drive while I relax." Her voice was mellow and soft, already fading into a yawn. "Next time we'll bring my car." It was the last thing she said before falling asleep.

Austin nudged her awake when they reached her house. She opened her eyes and regarded him groggily. "I must have fallen asleep."

Austin thought he'd never seen her more lovable. Grinning, he said, "About an hour ago."

Rubbing her eyes, she said, "How was the drive?"

"The company was good."

"Now I'm embarrassed."

He touched her cheek with his fingertips. His eyes were filled with warmth as he studied her face. "I love having you next to me."

She was alert enough now to sense the change between them, the sudden sexual tension, the intensity of emotion.

"Austin . . ."

"You're going to tell me that you're not going to invite me in." It was half statement, half question, and his voice held more disappointment than ire.

She caressed his cheek with her fingertips. Unshed tears shone in her eyes. "It was special at the beach."

"Yes," he whispered.

"I've never told anyone what I told you. Not all of it, all at once."

His arms encircled her, drawing her next to him. "I'm flattered that you shared it with me. It's as though you've given me a gift."

Snuggling her cheek against his chest, she said, "I feel so very close to you, as though you know everything there is to know about me."

"I don't know what side of the bed you sleep on."

He felt her tense, gently stroked her hair with his hand. "You can trust me, Shelby. I would never throw you away."

"I think . . ." She hesitated a long time before finishing the thought. "I think I'd like to give you that kind of trust another time." After another long pause, she said, "It's been a long day, Austin. So much happened that was . . . we agreed on the word, special. I'm still reeling with it. I need some time to absorb it. Maybe you do, too."

"No, Shelby. I don't need any more time. I want you and I need you. I'm ready to be with you right now." Sighing, he took his arms from around her and pulled the keys from the ignition. "But if you need the time, there's nothing I can do except wait." *And hope I don't die of frustration in the meantime.*

He got out of the car and opened the trunk to take out Shelby's bags. Shelby felt numb, and a bit hollow inside. Had she really asked him to leave? Was he actually going to leave her?

He carried her bags to the porch, then walked her to the door. He kissed her one last time, drawing her into his embrace, pulling the length of her body against his, wishing he didn't have to let go of her. "Are you sure?" he whispered.

She was functioning now only on instinct, because she no longer could think logically. He was still holding her, still touching her. His body was lean and warm and strong. His strength was seducing her, his desire was calling out to her, rousing some similar force in her. She could feel herself slipping, surrendering.

But I'm not ready, she thought, desperately clinging to control. *I'm tired and confused.* She wanted to wrap up the day with him and store it in some safe place forever, to treasure. "I'm sure." There. It was said. It was irrevocable this time.

"If we'd been alone at the beach house?" he asked. She shook her head slowly against his chest. "I don't know."

But she knew, and so did Austin.

It was the only thing that gave him the courage to leave.

Chapter Twelve

"Our Caesar photographs well, doesn't he?" Ramon Caesar said, spreading his hand in the air over the color photos on his desk.

"Exceptionally well," Shelby agreed, looking down at twelve images of Austin, "especially when you consider that he isn't a professional model."

"That's the reason I called you as soon as I got the proofs," Mr. Caesar said. "Do you think your Mr. Hastings could be enticed to become a professional?"

Shelby slowly settled into the chair in front of Caesar's desk. "What did you have in mind?"

"If these photos were good enough, I was planning on using one of them in a newspaper ad. They're good enough, but the advertising agency tells me I need a model's release to use them. Will this man Hastings agree to sign one?"

"That shouldn't be a problem," Shelby said. "He's supposed to pick up his check tonight. I'll ask him then." The thought of seeing Austin sent a shiver of anticipation down Shelby's spine. She had plans for the evening. If Austin thought Saturday at the beach was special, wait until he saw what she had in store for him tonight!

Mr. Caesar tapped a pencil on the desk nervously, then laid it down on his blotter. "Actually," he said. Shelby blinked and forced her attention on what he was saying. "I'd like to get a little more from Hastings than just a release for these photos. This oddball scheme of yours has been well received, and I'd like to exploit it. How do you think Hastings would do in front of a television camera?"

"Television?" she asked incredulously.

"If he looks as good on video as he does in these photographs, I want him to become the official spokesman for Caesar's Office World." He paused, studied her shrewdly and grinned. "I've never seen you speechless, Shelby."

"I'm speechless now, Mr. Caesar."

"Problem?"

"Not with the idea. I'm just not sure how Austin would feel about television. This whole thing has been a temporary sideline with him. He's an engineer, you know."

"Didn't you say he's currently unemployed?"

"Between jobs," she said defensively. "I'm sure he'll be finding something soon. He talked to someone about a job last night, as a matter of fact, and he was supposed to go for another interview today."

"We'd better grab him quick, then. Frankly, I don't see why he couldn't do both. We could work around his schedule."

Shaking her head, Shelby said, "I really don't think he's—"

"It could be very lucrative for him. A rare opportunity. No telling where it would lead. I would insist that he not play the part of Caesar for anyone else, but the contract wouldn't have to preclude his doing other work. It could open a whole new door for him." Reading the skepticism on her face, he said, "At least talk to him about it. Or I could schedule an appointment with him, if you'd prefer."

"I think I'd better handle it," Shelby said.

Mr. Caesar grinned. "Frankly, so do I. Something tells me you have more influence with him than I would have."

So Mr. Caesar had picked up on the chemistry between them, just as David had. *Why don't you write it across your fore-*

head, Shelby, and save everyone the trouble of speculating? Shelby Thurston loves Austin Hastings. She choked unexpectedly. *Loves?*

"Are you all right?" Mr. Caesar asked solicitously.

"Just a speck of dust or something," she said.

Mr. Caesar pushed one of the buttons on his state-of-the-art intercom. "Mary," he said, "can you bring in a glass of water for Miss Thurston?"

Candles. Wine chilling in a bed of ice. Soft music on the stereo. Dinner, consisting of grapes and cheese, on a crystal plate in the refrigerator. After checking each detail one last time, Shelby slipped off her silk robe and pulled the white gown over her head, careful not to disturb the pageboy hairstyle she'd worked on so diligently. The sandals were next, gold sandals with ankle straps, suitable for an Egyptian queen awaiting a Roman ruler.

The chime of the doorbell vibrated through the duplex and every anticipation-charged nerve ending in Shelby's body. Trembling fingers picked up her perfume atomizer and puffed a cloud of her favorite fragrance into the air. She passed through it on the way to answer the door, feeling every bit the seductress.

She opened the door slowly and stood where Austin could see her. His reaction was what she'd hoped for: a gasp of surprise, an appreciative appraisal and, finally, a look of approval in his eyes. She let the smile form on her face slowly, gradually transforming her features from the cool elegant attitude of a queen to the warm welcome of a flesh-and-blood woman. "Come in," she said, her voice husky as it passed through a throat suddenly dry from anticipation.

Austin immediately perceived the aura of seduction as he entered the living room, breathing in the scent of Shelby's perfume. A cluster of votive candles in elegant little holders winked brightly on the coffee table, their reflected flames dancing in the stemmed crystal wine goblets waiting to be filled with the rosé chilling in the bucket.

Shelby followed his gaze to the table, waited for him to turn his attention to her again. "Would you like a glass of wine?" she asked, her eyes large and liquid with emotion.

Austin caressed her shoulders with his hands and smiled at her. "Do you know I love you?"

The seductress was shy, suddenly. A flattering blush rose in her cheeks as she nodded. Austin kissed her briefly on the lips. "I'll open the wine."

Silently they had reached an understanding: It will happen. And an agreement: There's no need to rush.

Austin removed the cork from the bottle while Shelby fetched the fruit and cheese from the refrigerator and opened a box of sesame crackers. Sitting on the floor, they sipped wine and nibbled at the finger foods. Sexual tension crackled between them, and they savored the sweet anticipation.

Lifting his glass, Austin looked into the fathomless depths of Shelby's eyes and said, "To you, because you are so incredibly beautiful."

Their glasses touched with a melodic tinkle. "To good things to come," Shelby said. Austin's senses reeled with the promise of the toast. His nerves jangled with the intensity of his need for her. Studying her face, relishing the passion smoldering in her dark eyes, he wondered how much longer he could hold back and let the tension continue to build between them.

Shelby leaned her head back, resting the crook of her neck against the rounded edge of the sofa, giving him a splendid view of her throat. His eyes trailed the elegant length of it down to her chest, and further still to the cleavage tantalizingly exposed by her gown. He imagined kissing her there, feeling the swell of her breasts under his lips.

"Tell me about the job lead. Is it a good job?"

A knot formed in Austin's throat. It was one topic he'd been hoping to avoid. "It's an excellent job," he said without expression.

"Challenging work, good benefits, perks?"

Twisting closer to her, he slipped his arm across her, letting his hand settle on her waist. His cheek pressed against hers. The corner of his lips touched the corner of her mouth. "All that," he said, and felt the tremor of expectation that shuddered through her as he moved to claim her lips in a wine-tinged kiss. When he pulled away from her, grazing his lips across hers one last time to soften the shock of parting, they had reached a new plateau of awareness. Still, they were in no hurry, preferring to let the tension build slowly to ultimate fulfillment.

A trace of panic colored the excitement coursing through Shelby. She'd sent him a message loud and clear, and he'd gotten it, but she wasn't quite sure what to do next. Her experience in seduction was too limited. She felt the desire growing in her, building quickly. But the moment of truth was still far enough away that she felt a bit self-conscious because of her inexperience, her lack of finesse. What type of small talk did one make in the middle of a seduction? Why couldn't she think of anything clever or suggestive to whisper in his ear?

Plucking a grape from the cluster on the plate, she touched it to Austin's lips. "Hungry, Caesar?"

Fighting for control, Austin opened his mouth and felt the grape slide past his lips, his teeth, and tasted the explosion of flavor on his tongue as he crushed it against his palate. She fed him another, then bit a cube of cheese in half, keeping it in her mouth, chewing it slowly while she pressed the other half to his lips. He took it in his mouth, and holding her hand next to his face, nipped at the tips of her fingers with his teeth. Then he kissed her palm, flicking at the softness with his tongue.

She sighed, and he pulled her hand to the floor on the far side of him so that she was leaning over him, across his chest. He drew his knees up behind her to support her while his arm snaked around her. The fullness of her breasts swelled against his chest, and he thought the exquisite torture of waiting might drive him to madness.

His thumb traced the shape of her lips teasingly, and then his tongue followed the same delicate, delicious line, tasting traces of wine and the shattering sweetness that was Shelby. Forcing himself to draw back, he ran his forefinger over the planes of her face, the curve of her cheek. "Was it hard to get your hair to do this?" he said, rubbing a strand of it between his fingertips.

"Not really," she murmured. *Help me, Austin,* she thought. *I need you, but I'm scared. Please understand me.*

He saw the plea in her eyes and understood it. The skirt of her dress was slit to the knee on the side and had crept higher when she sat down. He rested his hand on her knee a moment, then slid it higher to caress her firm, smooth thigh.

Shelby stretched her arms over his shoulders and spread her fingers over the back of his neck. She felt like screaming for release from this mounting tension. She had to say something, anything to relieve it. "Will you interview for it?"

Austin looked at her uncomprehendingly. "For what?"

"The job the headhunter told you about."

He tensed. The job was the one subject Austin didn't want to discuss now. He wanted to wait until later, when their commitment was made and they were basking in the languid aftermath of pleasure. Then perhaps he would be able to broach that subject. He wanted to brand her with his love-making first so she would understand that they were too good together to risk tearing apart. What was the line in the marriage vow—putting asunder? That's what he didn't want, that they would be put asunder.

"Austin?" she prompted.

He shook his head to clear it. "I'm sorry." He grinned guiltily. "I wasn't concentrating on what you said."

"I asked if you were going to interview for the job the headhunter told you about."

"Yes," he said, "I've already interviewed for it."

Sensing his withdrawal, the change in his attitude, Shelby felt a stab of fear, and felt as though she'd lost something essential. She wanted to draw him back to her, onto the spiral of sensuality they were climbing together.

Leaning forward, she kissed his neck and then traced his ear with her tongue. A deep, guttural sound not unlike a growl formed in his throat, and she knew she'd drawn him back. "Did you say something?" she whispered, letting one hand slide to his chest and rest there, feeling the pulse of his quickened heartbeat under her palm, feeling, in her own chest, her own heart racing with the same excitement.

"God, I want you," he said raggedly, lowering his shoulders to the floor and pulling her along with him, over him. The hand that was on her thigh moved up, came to rest over the thin silk of the panties on her hip.

Shelby shuddered in surprise and delight as the heat of his fingers penetrated the thin cloth, and an answering warmth spread throughout her body, stirring the voracious need inside her. Still, she wanted to prolong the sweet, terrible, torturous anticipation. Very slowly she lowered her head to caress his lips with the tip of her tongue.

His hand left her hip and moved higher to glide over her waist and then encircle her breast through the soft fabric of her dress. She gasped, sighed, kissed him fully, running her fingers through his hair as her lips met his in a sensuous kiss.

When she lifted her head and moved away from him she looked at him through vision blurred by passion, and smiled into eyes that were regarding her with awe and affection.

Austin shifted to his side and propped his head on his elbow. She followed suit, so that they were lying parallel to each other, their bodies close but not touching except where Austin's hand had settled cozily, possessively on her hip on the outside of her dress. "Now tell me about the job," she said softly, knowing instinctively there was little time left for conversation before anticipation gave way to action.

His features hardened, his eyes narrowed, he sat up and leaned against the couch, as though he felt a need to distance himself from her. "Are you playing games with me, Shelby?"

A whispered, "No," was all she could manage, but she continued shaking her head in denial of some unspoken charge he seemed to be hurling at her.

"How much do you know about it?" he demanded.

Something had gone very wrong between them. The anticipation was gone, leaving only frustrated desire. "I don't know anything about it," she said. "Nothing except what you told me. What's wrong, Austin? Why are you doing this? What do you suspect me of?"

He withered. It was the only word she could have used to describe it. He seemed simply to shrink away inside himself, his features contorted with misery. He reached out for her, pulled her to him urgently, held her pinned against him the way he would cling to a life preserver in a turbulent ocean. "Oh, God, Shelby, I don't suspect you of anything. It's me. I was going to . . ." A defeated sigh shuddered from his throat, finishing the sentence.

He raised up, sat on the sofa and then pulled Shelby to him. "We've got to talk," he said. "About the job."

She nodded against his chest. "All right." He could hear the shakiness in her voice, the same type of tremulous fear that was eating him inside. He refilled their glasses, and they sat apart, not touching each other as they sipped their wine. Shelby kicked off her sandals and put her feet on the sofa, wrapping the skirt of the gown around her legs and hugging her knees. She reached out, picked up her glass with one hand and drew it to her lips, wondering how she managed to function normally.

"It's a good job," Austin said abruptly, staring at his wine, his voice slicing through the prolonged silence. "They need someone to run the shop, answerable only to the owner, to start out as chief engineer and be named vice president within two years when the president goes into semi-retirement."

He took a healthy swallow of wine and frowned. "I checked. The owner has two children. The daughter is an artist who owns an arts and crafts store and is married to a lawyer with no interest in the engineering company except on a retainer basis for contract negotiation. The son majored in microbiology and starts medical school next month. I guess that's why his dad decided to get some outside blood into the firm."

She said what they were both thinking: "So you wouldn't be faced with the same problem you had at Mason Engineering."

Austin nodded gravely. "I met the owner. He wants me to visit the office tomorrow to meet the people I'd be working with and supervising. After that, it's just a matter of working out the details."

Shelby felt as though she'd stumbled into a thick fog on a dark night. Why hadn't he told her right away? Why was he acting so peculiar about it? "Why didn't you tell me you had a job?" she asked. "What is it you're *not* telling me?"

He was leaning forward, staring at the drop of pale liquid in the bottom of his glass. "The job's in North Carolina," he said and waited without breathing for her reaction.

Her eyes revealed her every emotion. He saw all the things he least wanted to see: realization, confusion, fury. Those bright brown eyes flashed at him, accusing him. "You were going to sleep with me, knowing you were leaving tomorrow."

"Yes, but—" He tried to put his arms around her, but she pushed his hands away and, feeling the need to flee, leaped off the sofa and walked to the middle of the room, her back to him. "I trusted you," she snapped.

"It's not what you're thinking, Shelby, not the way you're understanding it."

She still wouldn't turn around, didn't want to see his face. "I understand perfectly," she said, thrusting her chin in the air in a gesture of defiance. "You weren't going to throw me away, you were just going to fly off and leave me. Pardon me if the difference doesn't make that much difference to me." She choked back a sob. "The pain is just as real either way."

"It's not what you're thinking. I was going to ask you to go with me. I don't want to lose you, Shelby. We could be together in North Carolina just as easily as here."

She spun around to face him. "What about The Shelby Agency and my family? What about the beach and the rainbows?"

"North Carolina's on the same ocean, for God's sake. And they have rainbows there, too."

"Not as often," she said.

"You could open The Shelby Agency there. You said the agency was your badge of independence from Thurston Enterprises. Think how satisfying it would be if you made it work somewhere people have never heard of Thurston Enterprises."

"I'm making it work here without relying on my family. Starting all over wouldn't be just a matter of hanging out a shingle and waiting for the clients to call. Sure you want me to go with you. You have a fancy job waiting for you." She frowned. "And I'd have a big fat zero."

"You'd have me."

"For as long as it lasted," she said coldly.

"I love you, Shelby."

"Then stay with me. You can get a job here."

"Not like this job."

"One would come along sooner or later."

"In six months? A year? While I'm waiting around having everybody pat me on the back and tell me what a raw deal I got with Mason?"

"You can be Caesar while you're waiting. Mr. Caesar wants to put you under contract for special appearances and television spots."

"Television?"

"Spokesman for the company in some commercials Mr. Caesar is planning."

He sniffed indignantly. "Oh that would really enhance my professional image, wouldn't it. Everywhere I went people would point at me and say, 'There goes the clown who wears the toga on TV.' That would really help me get a job."

"It could," she said desperately. "It really could, Austin. Celebrity opens doors."

"You ought to know."

"I'm not a celebrity. I'm a—" Realizing how lame it

sounded, she added, "Thurston."

"I'm not a celebrity, either, Shelby. Exhibitionism is not in my personality."

"But you're so good at it."

"There was no skill involved, just a halfway decent body and good manners." Stepping behind her, he put his hands on her shoulders. "The only reason I ever put on that ridiculous toga was to be near you." She jerked around to face him and glared at him skeptically. "You knew that," he said. "You had to know it."

"If you love me the way you say you do, you could do it a little longer to stay with me. And I could talk to my father about an engineering job. He knows—"

"I can't believe you'd suggest that to me, knowing what you know about me," Austin said sadly.

"I wasn't offering you a free ride, Austin, just a good word in the right places."

"Thurston-style," he said bitterly. "I got this job on the basis of my skills and work history. I'd never know that about a job I was referred to by your father. It's not fair of you to ask me to be less than I am. I played Caesar for you as long as I could. Now I have a chance to go back to being Austin Hastings. He's an engineer. A damned good one."

"You can be an engineer and Caesar, too. Mr. Caesar said he would put it in your contract that you could work around your regular work schedule."

Austin had thought nothing could make the situation any worse than it already was, but an ugly suspicion crept into his mind. "You and Mr. Caesar seem to have worked out my life pretty well between you. When were you going to spring this one on me? Does this little scene tonight have anything to do with that contract you two cooked up?"

Shelby's spine was straight and stiff as a pole. "I think you should leave now," she said quietly.

"Maybe I should," he said. "I'm finding it hard to concentrate on arguing with you since I've felt the merchandise."

"Too bad cold showers don't work for you. I'd offer you the bathroom."

Realization descended over Austin in a dismal cloud. They'd said things they didn't mean, and now they'd lost what they had been so close to finding. "I was going to ask you to marry me, Shelby."

"With our track record?" she snapped. "I'm not into masochism, thank you."

Austin's nostrils flared as he took a deep breath and struggled to control his temper. "You're right," he said. "It's time for me to leave."

She watched him stalk across the room and fling open the door. He hesitated for an instant, just long enough, perhaps, for her to call out to him and ask him to stay.

But Shelby was paralyzed by shock. Her voice wouldn't work. It was only later, after she'd heard the sound of his car become fainter as he drove away that she was finally able to move. A sob tore through her throat, the presage of the torrent of tears to come.

Chapter Thirteen

Austin drove aimlessly through the streets. Like the survivor of a catastrophic accident, he was numb with shock. He was not acting so much as reacting, and rote reaction took him to familiar streets and old haunts. He was vaguely chagrined to find himself in the vicinity of the Mason Engineering offices, and impulsively he pulled into the parking lot of a pub he and some of his co-workers at Mason had frequented. It was a casual place, clean, with a good selection of hot and cold deli sandwiches and fried vegetable appetizers. The bar carried the profits at night, though, and the waitresses brought complimentary munchies in napkin-lined wicker baskets to the tables when they came to take drink orders.

Austin took a table, ordered a drink and found the pay phone, hoping to catch Bob at home. No luck.

Austin scowled as he slammed the receiver back into place, feeling unreasonably angry that Bob should be somewhere having a good time while he, Austin, was in need of a friend.

On his way back to his table, Austin reached the profound conclusion that women were the ruination of men. If Adam and Eve were a parable, whoever had thought up the apple deserved a Pulitzer prize for zeroing in on universal truths.

The waitress brought his drink, but he was no longer in the mood. He signaled for his check, counted out four dollars onto the plastic tray and left the full glass on the table sweating rivulets of condensation onto a cocktail napkin.

His next foray into the night streets took him back to Winter Park, up picturesque Park Street and down the minor roads that lead to Shelby's duplex. Time had tempered his anger, restored his perspective, renewed the optimism that let him hope he and Shelby might still salvage the wreckage of their relationship and make something of it.

Though a light shone faintly through the front window, Shelby's duplex was still as death. He rang the doorbell, beat on the door, tried the lock, sat on the fender of his car and waited long enough for Shelby to get out of the shower in case that's where she was. Then he rang and knocked again. His only response was the lifting of a slat in the blinds in a window in the adjoining unit. *All right, Shelby,* he thought. *I'll leave. If you're in there ignoring me, I might as well give up. And if you're gone, it would be silly of me—and downright inconvenient—to get arrested for loitering outside your door and scaring your neighbor half to death.*

He drove off hoping she was okay, wondering if she was deliberately ignoring him, wishing he'd tried looking through a crack in her garage door to see if her car was there and wondering where Shelby might be if she was gone.

At that exact moment, Shelby was sitting in her family's beach house dismally counting the number of times his home phone rang without being answered.

She'd fled to the beach house to think, and after two days of thinking incisive, soul-searching thoughts, Shelby decided that she had retreated in search of security as well. The beach house was an old friend with familiar walls that shut out the world, and the beach was reassuring in its very constancy.

Armed with a cane mat, a solitary sandwich made from the last of the tuna salad she'd mixed at lunch and a can of cola, she followed the familiar foot path to the beach. She had not bothered with a swim suit, since she was not planning to swim, wearing instead her beach pants and an oversized surfer shirt one of the male Thurstons had left folded in a drawer.

This would be her last visit to the beach on this trip. Tomorrow she would get up early and drive back to Orlando to resume her life. She'd done a lot of thinking, some of it about Austin, most of it about herself. She couldn't think anymore. Now it was time to live again. All the thinking in the world couldn't straighten out the mess with Austin; only some frank communication between the two of them could do that.

It was dusk, her favorite time at the beach. She laid the mat as close to the water's edge as possible, sat down and stared at the surf. There were no rainbows today, since there'd been no afternoon showers, only skies of a deep velvet blue hosting cottony clouds and, in the west, what promised to be a beautiful sunset.

It was warm, but Shelby didn't care. She was here to make peace with the truths she'd discerned about herself and her feelings and Austin, truths that were so simple they were painful to deal with. Primary among them was that she was scared—scared of commitment, scared of change, scared to take a chance. She was clinging to the status quo, trying to change things around her to fit into the familiar, secure patterns she'd set for herself. She'd managed to face the truth of herself early on in her stay at the beach.

She'd faced the truth about Austin, too. Austin was not scared or selfish. He was strong and generous. She'd been too insensitive to realize how generous he was to play Caesar for her, how much he'd hated it, how much it had rubbed against his grain to be ogled and pawed. The fact that he'd done it to be near her wasn't selfishness, it was sweetness.

Austin wasn't perfect, of course, but as human beings

went, he was close to the top of the heap. And now he was ready to make a commitment, had made it, in fact, when he told her that he loved her. And all he asked was that she make a commitment, too.

That's what she was dealing with, really. Not whether she wanted to leave Florida and the social standing being a Thurston afforded her, but whether she was ready to risk finding out if Austin's love could satisfy her in a way that nothing else ever had.

Love was the easy part. Love just grew up inside a person of its own accord. It was commitment that was tough. Commitment required a conscious decision, deliberate action. The difference between love and commitment was like the difference between imagining a masterpiece and creating it.

She ate her sandwich and drank her cola, unheedful of and unheeded by the tourists. Afterward, she fed the crusts to the sea gulls, wondering if it was the same flock she and Austin had fed together. She took a long walk then, letting the water lap at her ankles and lick at the cuffs of her pants. It was dark when she returned to the mat, and the beach was deserted except for the occasional frenzied sand crab skittering across the sand. It probably was not safe for her to be there alone, but she stayed, oblivious to danger, watching reflected moonlight dance on the waves while her hair and clothes absorbed the ocean's night mist and her mind absorbed the serenity of the endless slapping of water on sand.

North Carolina was on the same ocean, he'd said.

The message machine was full of recorded messages.

Shelby's friend Lacey had called to make a lunch date.

Caroline from Mr. Caesar's office asked that she call Mr. Caesar soon about scheduling a video session.

Shirley from the glass company said that Mr. Hargrove

had received the contracts, signed them and was returning a copy for her files.

Her mother had called to say hello and tactfully suggested Shelby shouldn't be such a stranger at the ranch.

And, early on the tape, was a message from Austin, awkwardly saying he didn't want to leave without saying goodbye, that he'd talk to her soon. Later on the tape, his voice said, "I'm in North Carolina, and I've been trying to get you since yesterday. Call me, Shelby. I need to hear your voice." Smiling, she grabbed a pencil and pad to write down the number where he'd be.

Hastily she dialed it and asked for the room. A woman answered and Shelby felt her breath catch in her throat. "There's no one here by that name," the feminine voice informed her. "You might try the hotel operator, though. My husband and I checked in less than an hour ago. Maybe he was in the room before us."

She called the desk. Mr. Hastings had checked out the day before.

Crestfallen but hopeful, she turned on the message machine again. There were lots of hang ups, silent lapses on the tape that meant either the call was not important or it was too important to be handled by a machine. Finally, she heard the beautiful sound of Austin's voice again. "I'm back in Orlando. Call me." A pause. "If you don't get back to me before my phone's disconnected I'll call back and leave a new number."

His phone disconnected. He was really leaving, with her or without her.

He answered on the second ring, sounding perturbed. "Austin?" she said.

"Shelby? Oh, Shelby, thank God. I've got to see you. How about later, as soon as . . . excuse me, Shelby. I've got a minor crisis." She heard him say, "No. Don't pack that yet. I've got to vacuum before I leave. Oh. Well, if . . . sure, I can borrow one." He returned to the phone. "It's a madhouse here. The movers are running in and out and I'm trying to clean behind them. Damn! The doorbell's ringing. It's probably the real estate agent with the listing contract. Can I see you later?"

"Sure, Austin. But . . ." Suddenly she was talking to silence.

So Austin Hastings was dealing with movers and real estate agents and a condo to clean and his phone had just been disconnected. Well, he wasn't going to have to deal with this move alone; he wasn't going to have to deal with anything alone anymore. That was what commitment was all about.

She threw on her oldest jeans and the big old chambray shirt she used for painting and similar messy chores. Then she gathered up the supplies she'd need. In minutes she was behind the wheel and on her way to Austin's home.

The front door was standing wide open and Austin Hastings's life and possessions were spread out across the lawn and landing for the whole world to see. She didn't bother trying to shift the paraphernalia she was holding to knock, didn't wait for an invitation to enter. Austin was standing next to the bar that separated kitchen from breakfast nook, concentrating on a contract a well-dressed woman, who was obviously a real estate agent, was explaining to him.

"You might want to consider providing this repair warranty for the buyer," she was saying, and Austin, bless his smart little heart, was nodding politely but not signing on the dotted line.

Shelby cleared her throat, thoroughly enjoying the look of consternation that played over Austin's features when he looked up and discovered her there in her old clothes with a mop and bucket in one hand and a caddy of cleaning products in the other. "Mr. Hastings, may I speak with you a moment? In private?" she asked in a businesslike tone.

"Uh, of, uh, of course," he mumbled. Then to the agent, he said, "Excuse me."

The agent nodded graciously, and Austin followed Shelby to the back of the condo, dodging the movers who were carrying a heavy chest of drawers through the hallway. "Well aren't you going to say anything?" she asked, when it seemed he really was going to stare at her for the rest of eternity.

"I can't believe . . . what's this . . . ?" He threw his arms around her. "Oh, God, Shelby, I'm glad to see you!"

"That's more like it," she said, laughing and enjoying the feel of his body next to hers as he hugged her.

"What's with the mop and your clothes?"

"You didn't expect me to mop floors and scrub bathtubs in my good clothes, did you?"

"I didn't expect you to mop floors and scrub tubs at all. What's the idea?"

She looked up at him, relishing his handsome features and seeing the love in his eyes. "You need help, don't you?"

"I need you, Shelby. If I have you, nothing else matters."

"That's very romantic, but it's not going to get your place ready to show. Now, shall I start in the bathrooms or the kitchen?"

Austin still spoke as though dazed. "The bathrooms are in pretty good shape. The kitchen is a disaster since the packers finished."

"The kitchen it is, then. And you needn't look at me that way. The Thurston housekeeper was a harridan, and any Thurston offspring was fair game for the draft when it came to spring cleaning. So I know what I'm doing." She turned to leave, then looked back over her shoulder. "If you hold off on signing that contract, I can get you a reduced listing rate through Thurston Realty. And no matter what you decide, I wouldn't buy the repair warranty. This place is in pretty good shape, and it's a seller's market in Orlando now."

She wiped out cabinets, cleaned the refrigerator, sponged the counters, scrubbed the drip pans from the stove, scoured the sinks and, finally, mopped the floor. Several times she discovered Austin staring at her incredulously while she worked, but his attention was always usurped by some crisis with the movers. When the van finally pulled away, he sought her out and found her going from sill to sill with a damp cloth. "I brought my vacuum," she said. "It's in the car. You weren't planning on trying to clean these carpets yourself, were you?"

"There's a crew coming Tuesday. My neighbor's going to let them in."

"Then we're almost through."

Dutifully, Austin brought in the vacuum cleaner and vacuumed while she went through the condo one last time with a damp cloth and ran the mop over the bathroom floors. They rendezvoused, quite coincidentally, in what had been Austin's bedroom. Austin turned off the vacuum and said, "I see they managed to leave what I wanted them to leave." He looked at a lone suitcase sitting forlornly under a suit bag hanging in the cavernous walk-in closet. "I had to stop them from carting them off three times."

"Moving is a hassle. I'm certainly not looking forward to that part of it."

He cocked his eyebrow at her significantly. "Planning on moving sometime soon?"

Shelby was tingling all over. She wasn't sure how much longer she could bear this pussyfooting around. She nodded. "I've heard North Carolina is pretty."

"What made you think of North Carolina? The climate, the hills?"

"There's this man, you see, and—" She didn't finish the sentence. It was impossible to talk with Austin kissing her as though he'd been at sea for three years instead of in North Carolina for three days.

His lips left hers only long enough to whisper fiercely in her ear, "Marry me, Shelby. We can fly to Las Vegas tonight and fly to North Carolina from there."

"Tonight?" she said breathlessly.

He kissed her again, briefly, intensely. "Or tomorrow, if you want to have one of the Thurston family attorneys draw up a prenuptial agreement."

Shelby was finding it hard to think of anything beyond his Las Vegas remark. "A what?"

"You know, a piece of paper that proves I'm not marrying you for the Thurston family fortune."

"I never once thought you were after me for my money."

"I'm just trying to cover all the bases, Shelby. I don't want any doubt between us about anything."

"I've been thinking about this, Austin. All the doubt and the misunderstandings—they're just because we don't know each other, even though everything between us is always so . . . intense."

"Define intense."

She blushed. "I don't have to define it. I can feel it when you hold me like this."

"On my side or your side?"

"It kind of jumps back and forth."

Austin threw back his head and laughed a beautiful, hearty belly laugh.

"I'm trying to be serious," she said.

He forced a deadpan expression on his face. "What was your next point?"

"That once we know each other a little better, and certain . . . obstacles . . . are out of the way, we won't doubt each other anymore."

"That's very profound," he said, trying not to grin but finding it impossible to be serious when he was bubbling over with the joy of having her with him. "Did you come up with any other gems when you were doing all that thinking?"

"Only that I love you," she said.

"That's hardly an 'only that' if it's true."

"If it's true? You don't—you can't doubt that I—"

"Shelby," he said sternly. "Please shut up and kiss me."

She complied happily, loosening her grip of him only when he knew he'd been thoroughly kissed. "You'd better finish the vacuuming," she said. "If I'm going to Las Vegas tonight, I've got to get home and shower and pack."

"You want to go tonight?"

"You're not backing out, are you?"

"No. It's just so . . . sudden."

"It was your idea," she reminded him.

"I just . . . well, that obstacle you were talking about seems quite imposing at the moment. I thought . . ."

"We'll take care of that obstacle after the ceremony."

"Shelby! Have mercy on me. I'm a frustrated man."

"Unless, of course, there's time between my shower and the time we have to leave for the airport."

"I'm vacuuming," he said, flipping the switch and shoving the machine wildly around the floor. "See? I'm vacuuming as fast as I can."

Shelby called the airline as soon as they reached her duplex. "There's a flight in an hour and a half," she told Austin.

He shook his head. "We'll never make that."

"The next one is the midnight special."

He checked his watch. It was six-thirty. A smile crept over his face slowly, a smug, satisfied smile. "That sounds about right."

"We'd like two seats," Shelby told the ticket clerk, and supplied all the necessary information. Austin lunged for her when she hung up the phone, catching her around the waist in a football tackle and throwing her over his shoulder, fireman style.

Giggling as he carried her toward the bedroom, she flailed at his back with her fists and squealed, "I've got to have a shower first! I smell like pine oil."

His free hand patted her derriere gently, possessively. "You scrubbed my kitchen. I'll scrub your back."

"Sounds fair to me," she said, quite naturally sliding into his arms as he lowered her feet to the floor.